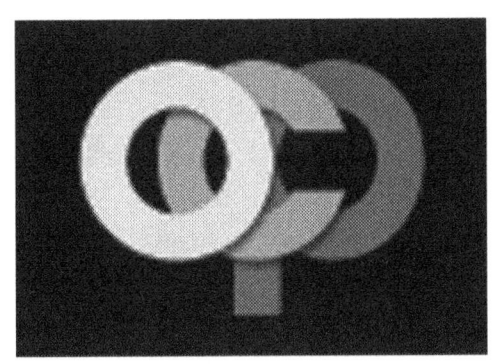

# OVERLOOK
# CONNECTION
# PRESS

# 2005

# NEW RELEASE
# CATALOG

Overlook Connection Press
PO Box 1934
Hiram, GA 30141

Bookstores and Libraries:
You can sign up for New Release E-mails and find out more title
Information at www.overlookconnection.com/ocpmain.htm

E-mail: overlookcn@aol.com

Phone: 678-567-9777
Fax: 770-222-6192

Our Distributors:
US: Baker & Taylor
US: Brodart
US: Ingram Book Company
US: Midwest Library
UK: Bertrams

# OVERLOOK
# CONNECTION PRESS
## Welcome to the OCP 2005
## New Release Catalog!

The Overlook Connection Press is happy to announce our special releases for 2005. This year we have a busy and exciting schedule. We have previously published fiction and non-fiction across the genre board. From the pool-hall vampires in Gary Raisor's *Less Than Human*, the unparalleled bibliography on Stephen King, *Horror Plum'd: An Intearnational Stephen King Bibliography and Guide* to Michael Marshal Smith's *Spares: Special Edition*. And we continue new releases in 2005 with more exciting fiction and non-fiction.

Tim Richmond's *Fingerprints On The Sky – The Authorized Harlan Ellison Bibliography: The Fully Illustrated Readers Guide"* encompassing over a decade of research into Ellison's body of work. Along with Harlan Ellison's invaluable assistance, this will be the most thorough volume ever published. Stephen King recently asked "Who's the scariest guy in America? Probably Jack Ketchum." (Ent. Weekly, Nov 19, 2004) referring to our release of *Off Season: The Unexpurgated Edition*. We just happen to have the sequel, *Offspring*, waiting in the wings for a Spring '05 release. F. Paul Wilson's Repairman Jack meets up with *The Last Rakosh* this Summer and follows up with *The Tery* this Fall. Philip Nutman's apocolyptic-zombie-fest *Wet Work* makes its limited edition debut in a special 10th Anniversary release with lots of extras not to be missed. We also have two very special short story collections, the first for both authors, *Matinee at the Flame* by Christopher Fahy, and *Smothered Dolls* by A.R. Morlan. Mort Castle's novel, *The Strangers*, currently in movie pre-production, is back in print. His *Cursed Be The Child* will also be released later this year.

This catalog features a special surprise, our first ever OCP Fiction Sampler! Here's an opportunity to visit with some of the upcoming releases, to take a peek inside at what you will find. I guarantee, it will whet your appetite for more.

Support our Specialty Book Stores! – listed in the back of the catalog. We appreciate your support of OCP books and products. So does our Specialty Book Stores – if you already frequent them… by all means, please ask them for any OCP titles. A few of our signed limited editions are *only* available through us and these stores due to the limited number of copies we publish.

Thank you for taking the time to look around our 2005 OCP New Release Catalog. Visit our releases online at: www.overlookconnection.com/ocpmain.htm year-round as we'll have more titles announced for 2006 and beyond soon.

Best,

Dave Hinchberger
Publisher, Overlook Connection Press

# 2005
# NEW RELEASES

# OCP FICTION SAMPLER

# A Hairy Chest,
## A Big Dick, And a Harley

## Lucy Taylor

**Release Date: January 2005**

**ISBN:** No ISBN for this edition - *A Hairy Chest, A Big Dick, and A Harley* is the "retitled" signed limited edition of *"The Silence Between The Screams"* (which is available for retail and libraries **ISBN: 1892950642** )

## A Hairy Chest, A Big Dick and A Harley is the Signed Limited Edition of *The Silence Between The Screams*

*Exclusively available ONLY to OCP Customers and OCP Specialty Bookstores*

*A Hairy Chest, A Big Dick and A Harley* is a collection of original short fiction and a reprint of a previously released novella. Her novella *Spree* has not been available for many years after it's initial printing sold out almost immediately upon publication. Now *Spree* and this collection of original short fiction is being published for the first time. It will be available in two hard cover formats under two titles: *The Silence Between the Screams* features the cover art by Rick Sardhina. This edition is available to retailers and libraries with an ISBN number in an "unsigned" trade hardcover.

Their are several reasons for the release in these two formats. First, *A Hairy Chest, A Big Dick and A Harley* is a story from the collection and the author's preferred title. The publisher, Dave Hinchberger of Overlook Connection Press, felt to reach a wider audience to go with the more subtle title. However Mr. Hinchberger, was in favor of releasing the "Hairy.." title as a signed limited with original cover art — only available on the limited — and giving Lucy Taylor readers and fans something special. Both Titles - *A Silence Between The Screams* and *A Hairy Chest, A Big Dick, and A Harley* feature the same text.

## Limited Edition Features found only in *A Hairy Chest, A Big Dick and A Harley* Are:

- Original and Cover Art for this Limited Edition
- A color Frontispiece of "A Silence Between The Screams" (without text) so you will have "both" covers in one volume
- Original Full Page Art for every story by Glenn Chadborn
- Signed by Lucy Taylor

*A Hairy Chest, A Big Dick, and A Harley* Signed Limited Hardcover of 1,000 copies     $44.95
*The Silence Between The Screams* - First Hardcover Edition   ISBN: 189295064     $39.95

**www.overlookconnection.com**

**Release Date: Spring 2005**

**Signed Limited Hardcover**     **ISBN 1892950707**     **$44.95**

# OFFSPRING

## By Jack Ketchum

THE STORY BEHIND THE GRUESOME LEGEND....
Twenty years ago....It shocked horror fans everywhere — Jack Ketchum's OFF SEASON, the brutal and harrowing story of an inbred family of cannibals in present-day Maine. Some readers were horrified, others outraged. Yet no one could put the book down. An instant cult classic.

THE LEGEND LIVES ON!
The local sheriff of Dead River, Maine, thought he'd killed them off ten years ago... a primitive, cave-dwelling tribe of predatory savages. But somehow, the clan survived. To breed. To hunt. To kill and eat. Now the peaceful residents, who came to Dead River to escape civilization, are fighting for their lives....

"OFFSPRING may well be the most horrifying book you will ever read."
### — Robert Bloch

"Who's the scariest guy in America? Probably Jack Ketchum, the outlaw horror writer whose terrifying first novel is finally available uncut from Overlook Connection Press. That would be *OFF SEASON: The Unexpurgated Edition*. If you read it on Thanksgiving, you probably won't sleep until Christmas. Don't say your uncle Stevie didn't warn you (heh-heh-heh)."
### — **Stephen King**, *Entertainment Weekly*, Nov. 19, 2004

*Features:*
- Author's Note
- Afterword Back to the Stewpot: On Offspring
- Original cover art by Neal McPheeters

Signed Limited Edition – Signed by the author $44.95

1/100 Sterling Editions. Silk book mark, Original Binding, Signed by author $85.00

52 Lettered – Full-grain leather, black wood box, with sliding door to access the book. Sliding door has pewter bones set inside. Each book and box crafted by hand. Bound in silk book mark. Unique endpapers. Signed by the Author. $500.00

OVERLOOK CONNECTION PRESS

www.overlookconnection.com

**Release Date: June 2005**

**Hard Cover Re-issue     ISBN 1892950553          $34.95**

# OFF SEASON

## By Jack Ketchum

"Only a novel of expert articulation and emotional truth can cast such a long shadow, and Ketchum's is both"

*— Publisher's Weekly*

"Who's the scariest guy in America? Probably Jack Ketchum, the outlaw horror writer whose terrifying first novel is finally available uncut from Overlook Connection Press. That would be *OFF SEASON: The Unexpurgated Edition*. If you read it on Thanksgiving, you probably won't sleep until Christmas. Don't say your uncle Stevie didn't warn you (heh-heh-heh)."

*—* **Stephen King**, *Entertainment Weekly*, Nov. 19, 2004

When *Off Season* was first released in 1980, it took readers by storm and sold over 250,000 copies! However, the original edition was edited and content was removed from the story at the publisher's request. The whole effect of the book was deemed to intense, in particular the ending — which is completely restored in this edition. The Overlook Connection Press has released this edition in it's original unexpurgated state for the first time anywhere. This the author's original vision, and now available in both trade hard cover and trade paperback.

We have a special introduction by Douglas E. Winter, who has championed this novel for years. Also an Afterword by the author Jack Ketchum. Original cover art by Neal McPheeters (cover artist for *The Girl Next Door*, *Red*, and *Right To Life*).

• Introduction by Douglas E. Winter
• Afterword by Jack Ketchum
• Cover art by Neal McPheeters

| Trade Hard Cover | ISBN 1892950553 | $34.95 |
| Trade Paperback | ISBN 1892950200 | $22.95 |

# OVERLOOK CONNECTION PRESS

**www.overlookconnection.com**

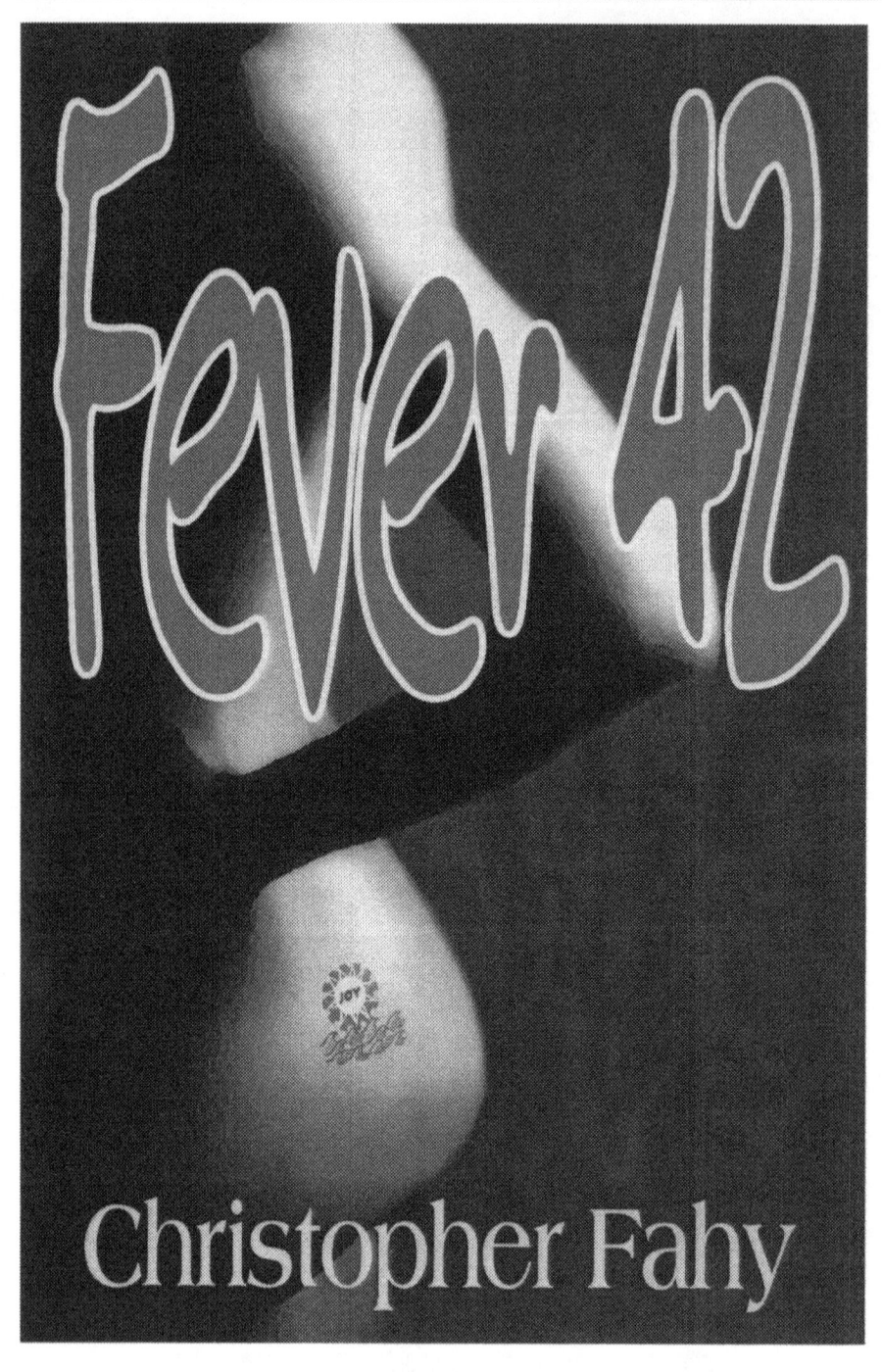

**Release Date: June 2005**

**Trade Paperback**     ISBN 1892950332          **$14.95**

# Fever 42

## By Christopher Fahy

"I thought that Chris Fahy's novel *Fever 42* was both wildly funny and surprisingly sad. The combination made me think of the early J.D. Salinger period. ...I think it will attract a lot of attention. Chris is a wonderful writer."
— **Stephen King**

"Ribald, erotic, hilarious, deeply serious and tragic, often all at the same time, *Fever 42* proves one of those rare books that restores our faith in the mainstream novel – and strangely, in humanity."
— **John Grant**, *Crescent Blues Book Views*

"... Gut-wrenching... Takes off like a drag racer howling down a quarter mile track."
— **John Robinson**, *Portland Press Herald*

"All the thrills and spills of a runaway mid-life crisis — from the safety of your armchair.. delightfully scandalous."
— **Michael Kimball**, author of *Undone* and *Green Girls*

"... A narrative that drives you like an out-of-control second-hand Dodge station wagon on a ride that makes you worry for your own strange trajectory."
— **Jack Ketchum**, author of *Off Season*

Ted Wharton, 42, a teacher at Whitman High in Somerside, New Jersey, lives a routine suburban life with his wife and kids. Disenchanted after fifteen years of teaching, going thru the motions at work – and home — he feels the clock is ticking. Then it happens: on the same day that one of Ted's colleagues drops dead of a heart attack, Joy, 17, a bright and stunningly beautiful senior in one of his classes, makes a play for him. And he puts up no resistance. Fully alive for the first time in years, he revels in his wild trysts with Joy – many at Whitman High. Living on the edge, obsessed with Joy, but realizing the ultimate disaster this will become, tries to end his relationship with her. Only to see his world spiral out of control.

A tragicomical tale of desire, deceit and betrayal, *Fever 42* is a thunderbolt of a novel, an unforgettable joyride.

| Trade Paperback | ISBN 1892950332 | $14.95 |
| Trade Hard cover | ISBN 1892950464 | $29.95 |

## OVERLOOK CONNECTION PRESS

www.overlookconnection.com

**Release Date: July 2005**

**Trade Hardcover      ISBN 1892950758      $29.95**

## The Last Rakosh

### A Repairman Jack Tale

### By  F. Paul Wilson

Repairman Jack has quite a following…

"Jack is righteous!"
   — **Andrew Vachss**

"The Tomb is one of the best all-out adventure stories I've read in years."
   — **Stephen King** (President of the Repairman Jack fan club)

"Call a plumber when the sink is clogged, the cops when you've been robbed, but when the you-know-what hits the fan, It's time to call Repairman Jack…"
   — *New York Daily News*

"F. Paul Wilson is a hot writer, and his hottest and my favorite creation is Repairman Jack"
   — **Joe R. Lansdale**

"Repairman Jack is one of the most original and intriguing characters to arise out of contemporary fiction in ages. His adventures are hugely entertaining."
   — **Dean Koontz**

Jack finds himself, and his friends, at a traveling carnival. During a look through the freak show, they come across what was believed to be extinct: a Rakosh. Jack had made sure that the Rakoshi were dead – exterminated. Jack style. But now, somehow, there appears to be evidence of an existing Rakosh. Or is it?

The Last Rakosh puts Jack back on the trail of this new mystery that will thrill and entertain… in Jack style.

Previously available as a short story, this version has been completely revised into novella length for this special publication.

First Trade Hard cover      ISBN 1892950758                    $29.95

**www.overlookconnection.com**

**Release Date: August 2005**

**Trade Hard cover**     **ISBN 1892950685**     **$59.95**

## FINGERPRINTS ON THE SKY:
## THE AUTHORIZED HARLAN ELLISON BIBLIOGRAPHY:
## The Fully Illustrated Reader's Guide

*Compiled & Edited by Tim Richmond*

## The most *complete* guide to Harlan Ellison's Life Work

- Book-Length Publications: Fiction, Poetry, Plays
- Short Fictions: Short Stories, Novellas
- Non-Fiction: Science Fiction Criticism, Theoretical Essays, and Reviews.
- Video and Audio Tape Dramatic Presentations
- Selected Secondary Sources: Interviews, Reviews, Articles, Biographical sketches, etc.
- ALSO: Cover art of most novels and collections, rare publications, foreign editions, reproduced here

This Book has been produced with Harlan Ellison's assistance to make it the most complete and informative guide to his life's work.

Tim Richmond has been working on this guide for over a decade. His discovery of rare articles and reviews by Ellison that Ellison hasn't seen in forty years! The last guide to Ellison's work was published in the mid-seventies. Now with the help of Harlan Ellison, and many others, Tim Richmond will bring you a complete guide to "Everything Ellison."

Trade Hard cover      ISBN 1892950685      $59.95

Signed Limited Edition – signed by Tim Richmond and Harlan Ellison
Featuring unique binding, endpapers, bound in book mark and more.    $100.00

Lettered Edition – Bound in full-grain leather, Featuring unique binding, endpapers, bound in book mark and more. Also features a DVD appearance of Tim Richmond and Harlan Ellison panel on "Fingerprints On The Sky." Unique hand-crafted slipcase. signed by Tim Richmond and Harlan Ellison    $500.00

*Limited and Lettered Editions available exclusively from OCP and Specialty Book Stores (Specialty Stores listed in the back of the catalog)*

**OVERLOOK CONNECTION PRESS**

**www.overlookconnection.com**

**Release Date: August 2005**

Trade Paperback    ISBN 1892950561    $19.95

# THE STRANGERS

## By Mort Castle

"*THE STRANGERS* offers one of the most unsettling and true representations of evil that you're likely to experience in a horror novel."
— from the Introduction by **Marc Paoletti**

"*THE STRANGERS* is one great scary book."
— *THE STAR*, Chicago Publishing Group/Hollinger Newspapers

You see him at PTA meetings, selling peanuts for Kiwanis, mowing his lawn. Michael Louden is your ever-so-average nice guy, your neighbor, your friend — except he wants to kill you and your family and your dog. He's the next door serial psycho, Jack the Ripper in Willy Loman's well shined shoes — and John Wayne Gacy in his clown costume.

And he's not alone. Michael Louden and others like him, Strangers, are just waiting for their moment of history — to destroy any hope of the future.

*THE STRANGERS*, Mort Castle's 1984 cult classic of hard driving horror, is coming back in print in a signed limited hardcover, and trade paperback.

*Features:*
• Introducion by Marc Paoletti
• Original Cover art by Erik Wilson

| Trade Paperback | ISBN 1892950561 | $19.95 |
|---|---|---|
| Signed Limited Hardcover – Signed by the author. Only 150 Copies. | | $44.95 |

*Limited and Lettered Editions available exclusively from OCP and Specialty Book Stores*
*(Specialty Stores listed in the back of the catalog)*

# OVERLOOK CONNECTION PRESS

**www.overlookconnection.com**

**Release Date: August 2005**

**Trade Hardcover**      **ISBN 1892950677**      **$37.95**

# Wet Work

## By Philip Nutman

Dominic Corvino – covert assassin, the CIA's top "wet work" specialist.

Nick Packard – a rookie cop about to undergo his baptism of fire on the Washington DC mean streets.

Two different men whose destinies are about to collide as Armageddon unfolds…

When a routine hit on a pair of rogue DEA agents goes horribly wrong in Panama, Corvino discovers not only has his team been betrayed from within, but he, too, is marked for death.

For Packard, his first day on the job rapidly descends into Hell on Earth when a domestic disturbance turns into a blood-soaked nightmare.

As a plague sweeps across the globe, turning normally non-lethal diseases fatal, the dead begin to revive.

Violence-crazed and hungry for flesh, they are everywhere. And as their troops increase in size – and appetite – a new order is steadily established from coast to coast…

A new order that leaves no room for the living.

"What Anne Rice did for vampire fiction, Philip Nutman has done for the zombie genre…an impressive first novel."
— **John Scoleri**, *The Horror Factory*

"The Genre is much enriched by his insight and creativity."
— **Clive Barker**, Author of *Abarat* and the *Hellraiser* series

"Nutman's style is crisp, frenetic, and vicious."
— **t. Winter-Damon**, *Nova Express*

Philip Nutman is an award nominated novelist, acclaimed short story scribe, screenwriter, journalist and comic book scripter, he has moved effortlessly between mediums over the last twenty years, weaving compelling macabre narratives. The author of nearly three dozen short stories, which have appeared in prestigious anthologies including *Book of the Dead*, *Splatterpunks!*, *Borderlands 2*, *Darklands*, and *The Year's Best Horror Stories XIX* and *XX*, to mention only a few, he is a four-time Bram Stoker Award nominee and a two-time finalist.

The most acclaimed novel of epic terror since *The Stand* returns to print in a special tenth anniversary hard cover collector's edition exclusively from The Overlook Connection Press.

*Wet Work* 10th Anniversary Special Edition Features:
• Introduction by Douglas E. Winter
• Wet Work – the original short story
• Blood, Guts, and Bullets – an Afterword by Philip Nutman

| | | |
|---|---|---|
| Trade Hard Cover | ISBN 1892950677 | $37.95 |
| Signed Limited Edition – Signed by Philip Nutman - Only 500 Copies | | $44.95 |
| 1/26 Lettered Edition – Full Grain Leather, silk book mark,.unique endpapers Signed by the author. | | $300.00 |

*Limited and Lettered Editions available exclusively from OCP and Specialty Book Stores*
*(Specialty Stores listed in the back of the catalog)*

**OVERLOOK CONNECTION PRESS**

**www.overlookconnection.com**

# Smothered Dolls

## A. R. Morlan

**Release Date: September 2005**

**Trade Hard Cover**     **ISBN 1892950715**     **$37.95**

# Smothered Dolls

## By A. R. Morlan

A.R. Morlan is a prolific short story writer whose first collection, *Smothered Dolls*, was long overdue to be collected in one volume. A.R. Morlan's work has been published in dozens of magazines and anthologies of horror, science fiction and fantasy. Over two decades of fiction have been looked at, poked and prodded, until we came up with what we feel is a well-rounded collection of this author's work. From the intimately disturbing title story *Smothered Dolls*, and *Powder* (this story is featured in the Fiction Sampler in this catalog), to the amazing and intense *The Second Most Beautiful Woman In The World*. Many rare and unpublished works appearing here together the first time.

A.R. Morlan is the author of *The Amulet*, and *Dark Journey*. Her short fiction has appeared many times in magazines such as *The Twilight Zone*, *The Horror Show*, *Night Cry*, *Weird Tales*, *Eldritch Tales*, and *Grue*. She has also appeared in the anthologies *The Years Best Fantasy and Horror*, *Obsessions*, *Cold Shocks*, *The Hot Blood* series, *Shock Rock 2*, *Lethal Kisses*, *Vanishing Acts*, and many more.

| | | |
|---|---|---|
| Trade Hard Cover | ISBN 1892950715 | $37.95 |
| Signed Limited Edition. Only 500 Copies. | | $44.95 |
| 1/26 Lettered Editions. Bound in full-grain leather, with a bound in silk book mark, unique endpapers and signed by the author. | | $300.00 |

*Limited and Lettered Editions available exclusively from OCP and Specialty Book Stores (Specialty Stores listed in the back of the catalog)*

**OVERLOOK CONNECTION PRESS**

**www.overlookconnection.com**

**Release Date: October 2005**

**Trade Paperback**     **ISBN 1892950731**     **$19.95**

# Matinee At The Flame
## By Christopher Fahy

We're about to release upon the fiction world Christopher Fahy's first-ever short story collection of the fantastic, *Matinee at the Flame*. Christopher Fahy's novel *Fever 42* was released to major critical acclaim last year. On the heels of that acclaim, we're about to let you see another side of Christopher Fahy, who Stephen King says ".. is a wonderful writer." *Matinee at the Flame* will take you on many different genre trails. From the *Twilight Zone* tempered title story, to stories of horror, science fiction, and the fantastic such as: *The Blumberg Variations*, *Night Watch*, *The Man in Black*, *A Special Breed*, *Want*, and *Carnival* which is featured in our Fiction Sampler in this catalog.

Twenty-One stories have been collected in *Matinee at the Flame*, over half of them appearing here for the first time. The previously published stories are being collected here for the first time anywhere. Artist Glen Chadborn has created full-page artwork for each story in this collection, as well as the wonderful cover.

Christopher Fahy is the author of fifteen novels including *Fever 42*, *Eternal Bliss*, *The Fly Must Die*, *Dream House*, *The Night Flyer*, and *Limerock* a collection of Maine short fiction. His short fiction has appeared in *The Twilight Zone Magazine*, *Cat Crimes*, *Predators*, *Night Screams*, *Gallery*, *Santa Clues*, *The King is Dead: Tales of Elvis Postmortem*, *Isaac Asimov's Magical Worlds of Fantasy*, to name just a few.

- Twenty-One Stories collected in this volume
- Cover and full-page interior artwork by Glenn Chadborn
- Limited Hard cover Signed by Author and Artist

| | | |
|---|---|---|
| Trade Paperback | ISBN 1892950731 | $19.95 |
| Signed Limited Hard Cover – Signed by the Author and artist | | $44.95 |
| 1/26 Lettered Editions – Bound in full-grain leather, bound in slik book mark, unique endpapers. Signed by Author and Artist | | $300.00 |

*Limited and Lettered Editions available exclusively from OCP and Specialty Book Stores (Specialty Stores listed in the back of the catalog)*

**OVERLOOK CONNECTION PRESS**

**www.overlookconnection.com**

**Release Date: October 2005**

**Trade Paperback**     **ISBN 1892950324**     **$19.95**

## The Tery

## By F. Paul Wilson

THE TERY

Heroes don't always look the part.

He was a tery, a lean, bearish creature with no name. The human soldiers left dead. Just another dumb animal on their extermination list.

But he didn't die.

Animals weren't the only beings on the list. Certain humans were marked for extinction as well. A fugitive band found him and brought him back from the brink. He became their pet, their mascot.

And still he had no name. He was simply "the tery."

He soon learned that these were no ordinary humans, and learned too that he was no ordinary tery. The humans had no idea that the creature they fed table scraps and patted on the head would soon turn their world upside down and change it forever.

By then he had a name.

THE TERY – A beauty-and-the-beast fable that only F. Paul Wilson could tell, full of wonder and horror, brimming with strange landscapes and hideous mutations from science run amok. An unforgettable tale of the extremes of the human spirit — of bravery and depravity, of innocence and evil.

- Foreword by F. Paul Wilson
- Cover art by Rick Sardinha
- Interior illustrations by Stephen Fabian

Trade Paperback             ISBN 1892950324                          $19.95
Signed Limited Hard cover – Signed by the author                    $44.95
1/26 Lettered Editions – Full-Grain Leather, Bound in silk book mark, unique end-papers,
signed by the author and artist                                    $300.00
*Limited and Lettered Editions available exclusively from OCP and Specialty Book Stores*
*(Specialty Stores listed in the back of the catalog)*

**www.overlookconnection.com**

**Release Date: November 2005**

**Trade Hardcover**   **ISBN 189295074X**      **$39.95**

# Stephen King is Richard Bachman

## By Michael R. Collings

This is the whole story of how Stephen King's Richard Bachman came to life, and when King finally had to "give up the ghost" and come forth with the truth – that he was writing under the pseudonym of Richard Bachman. This of course came about when the fifth novel, "Thinner," was released and a reader discovered King's pseudonym.

Now Michael Collings takes us from the beginnings of this unusual fiction side show of Stephen King's body of work, to what we understand will be the last Bachman release, "The Regulators." Or will it?

Updated and completely revised with new information and Richard Bachman releases since it's original publication almost 20 years ago.

Chapters Featured:
- A History for Richard Bachman
- Genre, Theme, and Image in Richard Bachman
- *Rage*
- *The Long Walk*
- *Roadwork*
- *The Running Man*
- *Thinner*
- *Regulators… and Desperation*
- Pipe-Dreams and Possibilities

Michael R. Collings is also the author of these OCP titles "*HORROR PLUM'D: An International Stephen King Bibliography and Guide 1960-2000,*" "*HAUNTINGS: The Official Peter Straub Bibliography,*" and "*STORYTELLER: The Official Orson Scott Card Bibliography and Guide.*"

| | | |
|---|---|---|
| Trade Hard cover edition | ISBN 189295074x | $39.95 |
| Signed Limited Edition – Signed by Michael R. Collings - Only 400 Editions | | $59.95 |

*Limited and Lettered Editions available exclusively from OCP and Specialty Book Stores (Specialty Stores listed in the back of the catalog)*

**OVERLOOK CONNECTION PRESS**

**www.overlookconnection.com**

**Release Date: December 2005**

Trade Paperback     ISBN 1892950723     $16.95

# Cursed Be The Child

## By Mort Castle

### The Past…

Her innocence betrayed, her body battered, her life destroyed, five-year-old Lisette lay dying. But hers was a will of uncommon strength for one so young, and even as she slipped into unconsciousness, she vowed revenge on a cruel world——even if she had to wait for an eternity.

### The Present…

Five-year-old Melissa loved her family's new home, especially the big basement to play in—and her new friend Lisette. Missy's parents said Lisette was imaginary, but Missy knew that she was very real. Missy could see and hear and talk to her. But Lisette made Missy do scary things, dirty things she didn't want to do, and when Missy told her to leave, Lisette wouldn't go away. Lisette had waited years for a child whose soul she could steal, and now nothing — not even death – could stand in her way…

"Mort Castle is a master of building characterization, setting, and atmosphere with an ecomony of words, a minimal body count, and an abundance of well chosen detail. This last quality he shares with Hemingway. Perhaps this is not a coincidence. In any case, it is also good."
— **Roland Green**, *The Chicago Sun-Times*

"Mort Castle understands something that eludes most writers, horror or otherwise: before there can be fear… and before the shadows in the corner of the room can have hold over you, there first must be a held breath of sadness and longing. (Castle's stories) achieve what all the best fiction should — they haunt you. In the soul. In the heart. In the night.
— **Gary Braunbeck**, Bram Stoker award winner

"Castle resoundingly steps on the podium with the likes of Stephen King and Dean Koontz."
— *Rave Reviews*

| | | |
|---|---|---|
| Trade Paperback | ISBN 1892950723 | $16.95 |
| Signed Limited Hardcover – Signed by the author - Only 150 Copies | | $44.95 |

*Limited and Lettered Editions available exclusively from OCP and Specialty Book Stores
(Specialty Stores listed in the back of the catalog)*

**OVERLOOK CONNECTION PRESS**

**www.overlookconnection.com**

# OCP Fiction Sampler

Page 35

Page 40

Page 44

Page 48

Page 56

Page 60

Page 64

Page 69

# MIRROR ME

## Yvonne Navarro

*Tuesday — October 3rd...*

"Say," Alice said. "How's Hannah doing? She looked in pretty bad shape when the paramedics packed her up."

Winnie shrugged. "She's okay. Ought to be home in a day or two. A good thing because—" She stopped and they both looked up as something thumped hard across the ceiling. There was a scattering of sounds, running, then unmistakably the sound of someone walking.

Alice glanced at Winnie. "Funny... I'd assumed you were taking care of the dogs."

"Not unless I can do it while wearing a respirator. Hannah's got some friend of hers doing it." It was the easiest way she could think of to explain it. Winnie stood there for a second, then turned and headed for the door. "Think I'll go check upstairs and meet this guy."

Alice looked delighted. "Guy? Hannah's got a guy?"

"He's just a friend," Winnie said automatically."

Still, as she stood outside and fished Hannah's extra key out of her bag, Winnie couldn't help fantasize a little. Hannah'd been through such a hellish existence, would it hurt the freakin' Universe to send a little happy in her direction? She let herself in but too late she realized the noise might not be coming from the dog-walking cop. It might be the other one, the asshole who'd tripped her at work. Hell, it might even be a burglar, or someone—

"Hi," said a male voice. "Can I help you?"

Her heart stuttered, then calmed as she stared at the guy standing at the end of the coffee table, a tug-of-war dog toy gripped in one fist. Knothead and Puddles whirled and saw her and she backstepped instinctively; before they could ambush her, the man dropped the toy and snatched at their collars, holding them fast.

"I'm Winnie," she said. "Hannah's best friend. I was down in the bookstore and I heard noises up here. You must be—"

"Greg," he said. "I'm looking after the dogs for her."

"Right." For a moment neither of them said anything and Winnie grabbed the chance to scrutinize him. Nice-looking, in an all-American sort of way— short blond hair going a bit toward the spiky style, yuppie-style glasses, blue eyes, maybe six feet tall with an athletic build. He could've passed for a computer geek instead of a cop, and maybe that was intentional— a bit too clean-cut for Winnie's tastes. But he looked safe enough for Hannah, and after all, he was a cop. Then again, so was that other moron.

"So," he began, "you—"

She sneezed.

«« — »»

By the time Officer Greg— as she'd already begun to call him in her mind— joined her on the sidewalk in front of Stars, Winnie had outlasted her sneezing. The "fresh" air of Belmont Avenue had cleared her sinuses of dog dander, doubtlessly replacing it with carbon monoxide. Now she could expect to sneeze once or twice every ten minutes for the rest of the day.

"You want to have a cup of coffee?" he asked. "We could go by the Diner—"

"Anywhere but there," she cut in. "It's not like I own stock in the place, you know?"

He grinned and glanced up the street. "What do you suggest?"

"I could do nachos," she said promptly. "Mexican place right up the block."

He motioned at her. "Lead on."

Winnie did, and it wasn't long before they were settled amid a colorful array of painted wooden tables and chairs and waiting for a iced teas, both deciding against the choice of early-afternoon alcohol. People chattered and waiters moved constantly— the place was a kaleidoscope of color and noise. Still, it made Winnie feel comfortable, sort of like the Diner but not, full of a protective bunch of people but without the spying, prying eyes of a fat, greasy boss.

"So you and Hannah are best friends," the cop said after the waiter had taken Winnie's order. "Known each other awhile?"

"Not so long," Winnie answered, and took a sip of tea. "A little over two years. We met at the bookstore."

He smiled. "Seems like a fun place."

That was obvious, so she didn't comment. Instead, she said, "It's awfully nice of you to do the dog-duty thing."

"I'd like to lend a hand with something else, too," he said. "I'd really like to find out who attacked Hannah in front of her doorway."

"If she knew, she'd tell you," Winnie said carefully. She picked up her water glass and took a sip, giving her eyes somewhere else to look besides into his.

"Really." Officer Greg folded his arms. "And what about you— if you knew, would *you* tell me?"

"Of course."

He leaned forward. "Because I get the feeling that there's a whole lot more going on here than she's willing to admit."

"Look," Winnie said impatiently. "She doesn't know who's doing this stuff, okay? If she…"

*Damn.*

Nothing stupid about this man— the way his gaze zeroed in on her, she knew her slip of the tongue hadn't gone unnoticed. "What I meant—" she began.

"No good." Before he could continue, a waiter appeared carrying a platter of nachos heaped high with salsa, sour cream, and jalapeno slices. Whew— saved by the taco chips. The cop gave her a few moments, loading up his own plate but fussily picking off all the sliced jalapenos.

"Don't like peppers, huh? You're gonna have a hard time getting Hannah to back off the hot food when you guys eat out," she commented.

Incredibly, Officer Greg blushed. "I don't know what you're talking about," he said. "I'm just watching her dogs while she's laid up."

"Isn't denial fun?" she asked mildly. "Some people—"

"Speaking of denial," he interrupted, "what did you mean when you said Hannah didn't know who was doing 'this stuff?' What 'stuff' would that be?"

"My tongue got twisted up, is all," she said quickly. She shoved a double-loaded chip into her mouth, effectively ending her answer.

"I saw the scar on her neck," he said abruptly. "And I read Dr. Tansey's report. Did you know her body is covered with them?"

Winnie stopped in mid-crunch. Sure, she knew about the scar on her neck— hell, everyone could see that one— and the one across her collarbone, too. But... there were more? Somehow she managed to mash the food in her mouth enough to swallow it, a mistake when it lodged somewhere in the middle of her esophagus like a wet lump of dough. "I knew about... a few."

"Where are they coming from?" Greg asked intently. "Who the hell is doing this to her, and why is she— and maybe you— working so hard to protect him?"

"She— *we*— don't know," Winnie insisted. "Listen, I already told this all to your partner. Wasn't that enough?"

Caught off guard, Officer Greg blinked. "You spoke to my partner? When was this?"

"So he didn't mention it?" Winnie's mouth twisted, but she managed to stop herself before her opinion of that jackass came out. After all, they were probably the best of pals, and Lord knows, she didn't need to get this guy pissed at her, too. "He came by the Diner on Sunday. I told him the same thing." She tilted her head at him. "You remember that part, right? That would be where *we don't know.*"

The cop surprised her by grinning at her sarcastic tone. "Yeah, I remember that. Vaguely. But I'm sure I'll forget it by the end of the meal."

"Then I guess we'll have to remind you."

"You do that." He swiped at his mouth with the napkin and stood, swiping the check off the tabletop as he did so. "In the meantime, I've got to head out— no, no, this afternoon snack's on me. Enjoy your peppers. And mine, too."

"Thanks." She reached across the table and plucked a finger-full of the ones he'd pushed aside from the edge of his plate. "Don't mind if I do. Waste is a terrible thing."

"True," he agreed. "I'll be around with the dogs if you get a sudden flash of recollection. Any idea when Hannah'll be released?"

"Maybe tomorrow, maybe not." Winnie frowned. "That doctor doesn't like her."

"I think it's more likely that she's worried about Hannah rather than something personal," Greg said.

"Aren't we all," Winnie said.

"Yeah." He threw a ten dollar bill on the table, then added another couple of bucks for the tip, unconsciously scoring brownie points. "We are. So keep in touch."

Winnie nodded automatically and watched him go, then almost laughed outright when she realized she'd been trying to imagine what he and Hannah would look like as a couple— what, suddenly she was having matchmaker urges? From the blush she'd seen earlier, Hannah didn't need any help with this one, although she wasn't at all sure how her friend would, or even if she *could*, handle a relationship with a guy. She didn't know all the details, but Winnie had the impression Hannah's growing-up times hadn't been so hot; the girl *never* talked about her past and that much secrecy usually meant a lot of pain and no gain in bringing it up. Unfortunately, it also usually meant a hard time in the here and now.

Winnie looked down at the table and saw that Officer Greg had also managed to drop one of his cards on the table without her noticing. She picked it up and fingered it thoughtfully. Had she really seen what she thought she'd seen that day a couple of weeks ago in the bathroom at Hannah's? So much had happened since then, Hannah's attack included, that it was hard not to doubt her own memory. The mental images she'd thought were so burned in her head were fading fast, worn away by the work and stress of everyday life, the recent increased worry about Hannah. Still, a few were hanging in there, unpleasant and, perhaps, unwanted—

*Standing outside Hannah's bathroom door, giggling over something inane, some stupid blond joke about a woman getting off a bus and walking down the sidewalk, not realizing her left breast was hanging out of her blouse. Hannah was listening and laughing around a mouthful of toothpaste, rushing through the ritual because she knew that even though the dogs were banished to their rug and the place was vacuumed, Winnie was apt to start spewing snooze at any second. She'd just said the punch line—*

*"And so she says to the cop, 'Oh my God, I left the baby on the bus again!'"*

*—when a thin line of red, shocking and growing wider with every slow-motion blink that they stared at it, appeared literally out of nowhere and swept across Hannah's right collarbone. Hannah dropped her toothbrush into the sink and winced, then slapped her hand against her shirt as the red spread through the fabric like a streak of scarlet paint. Her finger fumbled at the buttons and she peeled it away, revealing a fresh three-inch wound, weeping crimson tears.*

*"What the hell?" Winnie demanded. "How did this happen?"*

*"It doesn't matter," Hannah said grimly. She quickly stripped off the ruined*

*shirt and tossed it in the wastebasket. Lines of red dripped down her thin chest and she swiped at it with one hand, trying to keep it from reaching her bra. Her clean hand yanked open the medicine cabinet and pulled out a box of gauze pads. "Here— open a couple of these."*

*Winnie did as she was told, then watched as her friend took the wad of gauze and pressed it against the wound to slow the bleeding. "Hannah—"*

*"I can't explain it," Hannah said grimly. "And if you think about it too much, it'll do nothing but make you as crazy as I am." She slammed the door to the medicine cabinet hard enough to make Winnie cringe, then fixed her with a haunted stare. Hannah's voice softened. "So just pretend you never saw a thing, okay? It's just... easier that way."*

«« ———— »»

From MIRROR ME by Yvonne Navarro © 2004
Now Available ISBN: 1–892950–69–3

# OFFSPRING

## Jack Ketchum

## ONE
## MAY 12, 1992
## MORNING

She stood dappled in grime and moonlight beneath the drifting branches of the shade tree and watched through the window.

Behind her the others jittered.

She touched the screen with her fingertips. It was loose. Old. She rubbed her thumb and forefinger together, felt the fine grit of rust.

She concentrated on the girl inside. The acid-flower scent of her, riding high and strong over the musty-smelling couch on which she lay—even above the warm, grease-soaked kernels of grain in the bowl beside her.

The girl smelled of musk. Of urine and wildflowers.

The girl had breasts and long, dark hair.

Older than she was.

Her clothes were tight.

*They would hinder.*

The males pressed close, anxious to see. She let them.

It was important that they know what lay inside, though she would guide them when the time came. The males were younger and needed guidance.

But this was new to them, and thrilling. The lash of thin birch sticks across their bodies. For balance they would have to look carefully now.

She felt the diamond brush her chest, its cool gold setting, swaying from the dirty knotted twine.

The night was still. Crickets calling in the hollow.

*They watched the girl lost and deaf to them in the bright splash of voices out of the flickering light. And each, for a moment, as though brushed with the wind of one sudden mind, felt the baby asleep and alone above them in the thirsty dark*—their *dark, the dark of their elders, of the Woman and First Stolen.*

*They imagined they could see the child, smell the child.*

They only had to watch.

A single cloud had only to pass before the moon.

# 1:46

*Dammit, Nancy!*

Every light in the house was on again. Downstairs, anyway.

She turned the Buick wagon up into the drive.

*Girl must think I'm made of money,* she thought. *I bet the stereo's on and the TV too and there's no Coke left in the refrigerator.*

She was just a little drunk.

Her right rear wheel slid over the row of rocks and gravel and crushed three of the remaining tulips trying to survive at the edge of the lawn. *To hell with 'em,* she thought.

She'd crushed them sober too, half as often as not.

She cut the motor. Switched off the lights.

She sat there a moment thinking about Dean across the bar, ignoring her, drinking his Wild Turkey, her goddamn *husband* for god's sake looking right through her as though she were a ghost.

But that was Dean. Either you got nothing or else you got a whole lot more than you'd ever want to bargain for.

The nothing was better.

It was humiliating, though. And typical. Whether you lived with him or without him he was Mr. Humiliation. He got his kicks that way.

She took a deep breath to shake off the anger and opened the car door, reached for her old black purse with the .32 revolver in the zippered side pocket that she kept there just in case he tried to beat the shit out of her again like he had in the Caribou lot last Friday night, pushed away from the wheel, and got out. It was harder than it should have been. She'd never lost the weight after the baby. She guessed the beers didn't help any. The purse felt heavy on her arm.

*Fucking Dean.*

She slammed the car door. It didn't shut right on the driver's side. *I got to fix that,* she thought.

*With what?*

With Dean gone there was hardly enough money to feed her and the baby. That and pay the sitter one night a week. With the housework and the job, that one night a week—a movie and a couple of drinks, maybe—was a necessity now that the baby was finally old enough to be left for a while. But a barmaid made next to nothing in Dead River, and nobody tipped worth a shit. Whatever you had to say about the tourists, they tipped at least.

*One more month,* she thought, *till tourist season. You just got to hang in there.*

She stepped across the cracked macadam to the side door, sorting through her key ring for the house key.

She heard something thump through the open kitchen window. A Coke bottle, probably, against the too-expensive butcher-block table. Nancy eating and drinking her out of house and home again.

*I guess I could cut down on the beers,* she thought. *I could do that. Save a little money that way. I mean, what's important, anyway?*

*Me and the baby,* right?

She felt a flush of guilt.

Why did she always call her the baby?

Her name was Suzannah. Suzi. It wasn't always *the baby.* She remembered a time when she'd crooned the name. Now she hardly used it. It was as though the baby were just some sort of *thing,* another something in the way like the mortgage on the house and repairs on the roof or the faucet leaking down in the cellar.

She guessed Dean had screwed the pooch on that for her too. Like everything else.

For a moment she could almost cry.

She walked up the stairs and fit the key in the lock.

God*dammit,* Nancy!

She didn't need the key. The door was open.

She'd told the girl again and again —*keep it locked.*

Okay—so Dean was at the bar tonight. But he wasn't *always* going to be. He was going to drop by one of these nights when she wasn't home, when her car wasn't there in the driveway. And twice already he'd threatened to clean her out. Pull up in Walchinski's truck and haul away everything but the dirty laundry.

*I wouldn't put it past him,* she thought.

*I got to talk to this girl.*

"Nancy?"

She opened the door to the dayroom where the television was on without the sound—whatever goddamn good *that* was—and closed the door behind her and locked it. She kept on walking toward the kitchen. And the first thing she saw was the puddle on the linoleum floor seeping around the corner into the good hardwood floor of the dayroom—Coke, she guessed, coffee, something dark and flowing and *Jesus!* she was going to *murder* this girl—and stepping carefully to avoid it, she looked up and at the same time smelled the stink and suddenly what she was going to say froze inside her and so did the scream, so she could only stand there a moment trying to wrench it all into her at once like a single labored breath in a gale-force wind.

Two of them perched on the counter by the sink. Squatting, staring at her, eyes unnaturally bright. Their dangling arms covered with blood.

*Children.*

While Nancy lay naked on the butcher-block table.

Her body motionless. Pale.

Her arms already gone.

Her clothes lay scattered across the room. Her jeans beside the table—wet, brown and gleaming.

The cabinets were open, boxes and jars broken. Flour, bread crumbs, crackers, sugar, jams and jellies spilled across the counter to the floor.

Her arms were drying in the sink. Along with the dishes.

All this she saw in a moment, saw too that they were ready for her while her stomach boiled and the girl with the bloody hatchet and the two identical, filthy boys who had been holding Nancy's legs apart turned to her all serious and businesslike and not at all like the younger two squatting grinning on the counter.

She looked at the girl and, empty eyed, the girl looked back, and each seemed to recognize the other and what her presence meant here—and for a moment the object of their thoughts was the same, simultaneous, though the thoughts themselves were as different as blood and stone. The girl's thoughts cold, formal, almost ritualistic, an assertion of power, concerned that this woman should know everything that had happened here. Hers so suddenly urgent and up from so wrenchingly deep inside her that when her daughter's name swelled across her lips

(*"Suzannah!"*)

she knew Dean had done nothing to change what lay between mother and daughter, it was only a kind of exhaustion of her hopes, temporary, and that given time it would have passed. And knowing this, and knowing that there was no time, she felt her heart break then and there. So that when the smallest boy, the one she hadn't seen before, stepped out from behind the table with the white plastic trash bag pulled tight over the small, still, familiar form inside and held it up to her for her to see, she was already tearing at her purse for the revolver so she could blast them back to whatever hell they came from—and would have—had not the hatchet fallen in its fine arc to the center of her forehead and brought her instantly shuddering to her knees.

Blind to heartbreak forever.

«« — »»

From OFFSPRING by Dallas Mayr © 2005
Release Date: May 2, 2005 ISBN: 1–892950–70–7

# THE STRANGERS

## Mort Castle

There's always a wimp at a summer camp.

*The wimp at Camp Bethel, when Michael was 12, was named Alvin Burdell...*

It was a Tuesday night, forty-five minutes after lights out, and it was time to get Alvin Burdell, "Fat-Guts" whose inclusion on your team meant you automatically lost the race or the volleyball or softball game, the jerk who couldn't do one thing right but knew how to do a million things wrong, who got you sick just looking at all that wiggling blubber, and who, *just like a big fat baby!* wet his bed and woke up everyone in Cabin Three with that rotten stinking smell and his crying.

In his underwear, Steve Dawes led them, another boy aiming the penlight; they were the "Cabin Three Commandos" and the Target for Tonight was "Fat-Guts." Steve had appointed himself chief of the operation and no one had opposed him. He was thirteen and tough, a schoolyard bully on vacation at summer camp, always ready to do what he could to make life miserable for anyone weaker than himself.

More or less silently, the seven boys surrounded Alvin's bed.

Michael hung back as far as he dared. This wasn't for him, not his way to get involved with these *nothing people*—he had started thinking of them in that way since his talk with Jan—but he couldn't refuse to be part of it, either. He had to keep up the pretense, go on acting like everyone else, *the nothing people!* until...

Alvin was asleep. The penlight threw a yellow circle on his open mouth; a thick shadow moved as if something were trying to crawl out of his throat.

"Now!" Steve Dawes gave the order.

It was a smooth surprise as a pillow pressed down on Alvin's face, muffling his shocked cry, and hands held his arms. The blanket and top sheet were yanked down. Hands gripped Alvin's ankles, pinning him totally.

"Fat-Guts" was helpless.

"Yeah!" Steve Dawes said. "Now we fix him!" Steve was holding a can of blue paint and a brush. He kept saying, "Yeah," voice trilling with excitement, as Alvin's pajama tops were unbuttoned, the bottoms pulled down to his knees.

"Lookit that whale blubber!" Alvin's breasts were as bulbous as an over-developed woman's.

Steve laughed. "Itty-bitty prick like that. Way Alvin pisses, he oughta have a damn fire hose!"

Everyone was laughing, caution diminishing at the continuing success of the Cabin Three Commando raid. "Mowf, mowf!" came from beneath the smothering pillow. They laughed at that too. "Sounds like a harelip dog!"

"Move the light," Steve said. He took the lid off the paint can and squatted by the bedside. "We're gonna put a sign on you, Fat-Guts," Steve said. "Right on your titties. It'll say 'Porky Pisspot.' Then we're gonna paint your itty-bitty prick blue and tie you to the flagpole so when they raise the flag tomorrow, there's a big, fat surprise!"

Alvin Burdell heaved; he looked like a giant sea slug. "Mowf, woaa..." was his inarticulate plea.

The tip of Steve's brash trailed blue, a shaky line *P* on Alvin's right breast, then, next to it, an *0.*

Suddenly, there was a piercing sound—*Ahrkee*— a clack and a rattle.

"Now what the heck is this...?"

Light descended in a sharp yellow instant from the single bare 75-watt bulb overhead and froze The Cabin Three Commandos.

The boys scattered, backing to their own beds, turning and running, as Jan Pretre strode forward. The frightened excuses spilled out. "We weren't..." "...not doin' nothin'..." "It was just a joke, huh?"

Then Jan Pretre had Steve Dawes and Alvin Burdell threw the pillow from his head and sat up, blubbering hysterically,

"Hey!" Jan spun Steve around and Steve dropped the paint can. Holding Steve from behind, Jan cranked the boy's arm up between his shoulder blades.

Steve Dawes yelled, rising up on his toes, eyes bulging, his face as white as breakfast oatmeal. Then he started to peep like a starving baby bird, "Ohohoh..."

"Steve," Jan Pretre quietly said, "don't you know it's wrong to be mean to people? You shouldn't try to hurt Alvin." Jan pressed Steve's arm higher still.

"Ohohoh..."

Staring, Alvin was pulling up his pajama pants. Tears ran down Steve's cheeks and his face looked as if it were melting. "My arm, my arm, you're breakin'..."

"Now Steve," Jan said, "you really ought to apologize to Alvin. Let's hear you say you're sorry and that you promise never to be so mean again, okay?"

Each word of Steve's agonized apology was on a frantically ascending scale. Then he was begging. "Oh, please, my arm, don't hurt me, don't hurt me."

Jan released him. Steve staggered. Then, head down, working his shoulder, he slowly made his way to his bed, not looking at anyone. He crawled under the sheets, lay on his side, and shook with sobs.

"Alvin," Jan said, "there's an extra cot in the counselors' cabin. Come on, we'll get you cleaned up and you sleep there tonight."

When Alvin Burdell smiled, he looked like a jack o'lantern lit by a dozen candles.

On Saturday, after breakfast, Jan told Michael that he was taking him along with their "good pal," Alvin, on a special overnighter. Another counselor would take responsibility for Cabin Three that night. Jan told Michael that the overnighter would be a lot of fun.

Then he told Michael *how* they would have fun.

45

It was nearly sunset when they camped in the woods, far from Camp Bethel. Their site was near to a steep ravine, rough ground where the grass had lost the battle to stones and weeds.

Jan built a fire. He cooked beans, the open cans heated in the flames, and they roasted hot dogs on sharpened sticks.

"Having a good time, Alvin, old pal, old buddy, old chum?" Jan asked.

"Yeah!" There was a mustard smear along side Alvin's mouth, more mustard as well as ketchup on his T-shirt.

Alvin's hand splatted on the side of his neck. "Got that little stinker!" he crowed, reducing the mosquito's remains to gooey pulp and flicking it in the fire. "Lot of bugs tonight."

"Hey, no problem," Jan Pretre said, "You kill them. It's easy to kill them, isn't it?"

Sitting with his legs outstretched, Michael saw a rock within arm's length. He picked it up. It was egg shaped, the size of a baseball; he felt its weight.

Nodding toward the ravine, Jan said, "Really a beautiful sunset. Let's go take a look."

Alvin waddled beside Jan. They stood at the edge of the ravine. Jan pointed to where the pink ball of the sun seemed to rest in the V of a tree where two limbs joined.

"That's just like a picture postcard," Jan said. "All that pretty color. It's so fucking beautiful I could just shit."

"Huh?" Alvin said. He began to laugh. "Hey, Jan! I didn't think you talked that way. Hey! Shit!"

Michael got to his feet.

"Sure," Jan said. "I'm just the right kind of guy, you know, with the right language for the right situation. That's the way it is, old pal, old buddy, old chum!" He patted Alvin's shoulder. "You know what I mean, don't you, you fucking 'Fat-Guts'?"

"Hey, Jan, I know you're kidding around, but..."

Michael was running. He held the rock tightly, fingers shaped to it, and his arm was back as though he were about to throw.

Michael did not pitch the stone. Just as Alvin was turning his head, Michael planted his feet, locking himself to the earth. He swung his arm, snapped it forward.

He smashed the rock against the birthmark over Alvin's ear and there was a sound like a cantaloupe falling from a supermarket cart and smacking the floor. At the same time, there was another sound, similar to the crunching of the shell of a hard boiled egg.

*And there was yet another sound that might have been Michael Louden's heart.*

Alvin dropped to his knees, swaying. He said, "Dowah..."

Jan stepped in front of Michael, directly behind Alvin, and slammed his knee into Alvin's back. Alvin rolled down the ravine.

"Really a pretty sunset," Jan Pretre said. He told Michael to follow him, warning him to be careful; if they didn't watch their step, it would be easy to fall all the way down to the bottom of the ravine where Alvin lay.

Alvin was on his back, left leg twisted sharply beneath his rump, a pointed splinter of bone shredding the pinkish, oozing flesh of his right forearm. His eyes were wide open. The left side of his head seemed to be covered with thick pudding.

"You... hurt... me..." Each word brought a bubble of red spit to Alvin's lips.

"You are smart, old pal, old buddy, old chum," Jan Pretre nodded. "You are fucking perceptive." He laughed. "Alvin had a fall. Go boom. Looks like you broke your arm and your leg and cracked your little head so all your smarty-smart brains are leaking out."

Alvin's mouth opened and closed. A bright red bubble popped.

"What a bad, bad accident" Jan said. "I'm afraid old 'Fat-Guts' broke his neck, too!"

Jan bent, sank his fingers into the pudgy flesh under Alvin's jaws, and, gritting his teeth, twisted and jerked. There was a series of loud cracks, like a string of lady fingers, only louder, much louder.

Alvin's chest heaved once and his tongue shot out of his mouth, Then he let out a long, sputtering fart.

"And I thought he liked the beans," Jan Pretre said.

For two hours afterward, Jan talked and Michael listened. Jan told him about auras. Jan could see auras; he understood them.

Michael's aura, that of Michael—The—Stranger, the *real* Michael! —was very bright, very red. When Michael struck Alvin with the rock, Jan could not even see Michael's face for the brightness of it. Michael had been transfigured by the reality of himself.

And Jan told him what would happen next—and what would happen in the years to come—in the Time of the Strangers.

Yes, Jan was correct about what happened next. The police were understanding. It was evident that poor Alvin had suffered a fatal accident.

Because Alvin died twenty-three years ago, before it became fashionable and profitable for everyone to sue everyone else, the child's parents did not charge negligence against either the "good Christian camp" or Alvin's counselors. Oh, they knew how their boy had felt about Jan Pretre; all Alvin's letters home had lauded the counselor who had been so good to him, so kind and protective.

You could tell Jan Pretre was crushed; he could hardly stop crying. This was a terrible thing and he would feel guilty forever.

And that young man who'd been with him... that Michael Louden... The way he carried on, he must have been very close to Alvin. The poor boy would probably have nightmares over this as long as he lived.

«《—》»

From THE STRANGERS by Mort Castle © 2005
Release Date: August 1, 2005 ISBN: 1–892950–56–1

# WET WORK

## Phil Nutman

### ECZEMA

"You have no idea how important narcotics have been to the Company. They've financed major missions off of drug deals. In the 1960's they even tested LSD on our own scientists. One guy went crazy and threw himself out a hotel window. The deeper in you get, the more you realize how much it stinks. That's why I got out."

—Ex-CIA Operative

*Pain*
*whitelightwhiteheat*
*...what?*
*???*
*...*

*He is dead.*
*Yet alive.*
*And like Lazarus coming back from the beyond, opening his eyes and looking with*
*confusion into the face of Christ, Corvino is not aware of what is happening to him.*
*The first electrochemical impulses dance between decaying synapses. Then,*
*wrapped in total darkness, his body spasms as the second collision of thoughts*
*and memory clips slamdance him into consciousness.*
*I am awake, asleep*
*swimming*
*(drowning)*
*dreaming...*
*The MacDonald Douglas DC-3 comes in low on its drop towards the tarmac*
*of Washington National as it lowers over the Potomac, the sound of its engines a*
*subsonic scream of metal maintaining space above the ground, the slipstream ruf-*
*fling his hair as he turns, a voice uttering his name*
*muzzelfashpain*
*(??aaahhh?—)*
*—and he is in his apartment watching TV Dan Rather talking about the*
*unusual phenomena of Comet Saracen strange colored tail debris green blending*
*into—*
*—lighblastflash*
*(PAIN!!!)*
*and—*
*I love you she says Vietnam kaleidoscope opium hash acid*
*—I don't do that shit—*
*others stoned immaculate Doors Hendrix paint it black*
*—black*
*black*
*(paint it...)*
*bla....—*
*asleep*
*awake*
*swimming*
*drowning*
*(No!)*
*—reach for the ...*
*surface*

*(float)*
*so cold*
*cold here—*
*... in your arms*
*(???)*
*rise ...to the...*
*(surface)*
*Corvino*
*(who?)*
*swimming, drowning, reaching, climbing, reaching...*
*(WHATTHEFUCK?!!!)*


«« —»»


*He opens his eyes. Sensory awareness kicks in.*
*Blackness.*
*(I'm blind)*
*Panic surges through stiff muscles, cold body jerking against freezing metal.*
*(I'M BLIND!!)*
*Get a grip. Control the fear. Keep it together. Old habits... die hard.*
*In this case they haven't died, have just been in hibernation for a short taste of eternity.*
*Where am I? What?—*
*All he remembers is a small flash of light, then nothing.*
*He lifts his arms and touches icy metal. Pushing, he realizes he is in a confined space. A box of some kind.*
*A coffin?*
*He pushes downward and there is slight movement. Pushes again. Bright fluorescent light explodes, his eyes squeezing shut as the shelf slides open.*
*So. At least he isn't blind.*
*He counts to twenty, allowing his tortured eyes to adjust beneath the lids, then slowly cracks them open. Realizing he is in an institution of some kind, he struggles from the shelf suddenly aware of his nakedness and the white sheet covering him.*
*And sees the blood.*
*On the walls. The ceiling. The floor.*
*Then the bodies.*
*A doctor, his white coat gore-soaked, bullet holes peppering his torso. A headless naked man lying across the doctor's legs. And the blasted body of an E.M.S cop who looks as if he'd blown his brains out judging by the position of the M-16 lying beside him.*
*Reality*
*—flipped, decaying cells trying desperately to recall what has happened.*
*A dead woman. Naked, peeled of flesh.*

# FLESH

Before the city drops into the night,
Before the darkness, there's one moment of light,
It's when everything's clear,
The other side seems so near...

—Jim Carroll


"You can't say it's wrong to kill.
Only individual standards make it right or wrong."

—Executed killer Melvin Rees, 1959

*It's a good night for a kill.*

Dominic Corvino stood on the balcony of the two-story stucco house, smiling tersely at the thought as he savored a cigarette.

Twilight in Panama City blazed unusually bright with the glowing orb of Comet Saracen hanging heavily near the horizon. The emerald luminescence of its long tail bleached the magenta sunset an eerie hue, casting traces of shadow on his deep-set features.

He admired the comet's unearthly allure. The celestial body's presence felt both ironic and appropriate. In ancient times, men hailed comets as harbingers of doom; they imagined the tail to be the shape of a sword, the circle of haze to be a decapitated head. That grotesque image seemed an apt metaphor for what, in just over fifteen minutes, would happen in the house across the street.

Corvino stretched back against the wall. His lean body bristled with a familiar, comfortable tension as he anticipated the scenario. On one level every assignment played the same: get in, hit the target, get out. Each sortie was planned to create a T'ai Chi-like effect—minimum force to achieve maximum effect, manipulating your opponent's strength against him. A short, intense burst of the killing art and a swift, silent departure. Poetry writ in bloody motion. Still, on another level, every hit was unique. Each location proved problematic in its own fashion.

As usual, he arrived a stranger in a strange land, but masquerading as a local came with the territory. Sometimes—like that KGB defector mission in Sweden, back in the mid-eighties— physical attributes made it more difficult, but, in this case, his dark Italian features blended ideally into the Latin American environment.

A pang of apprehension gnawed at him though. Why? His imagination? Yet he could sense an undercurrent of electricity in the air, like the sharp taste of ozone before a storm, and the feeling had dogged him since his arrival four hours ago. Caution came with the job. Maybe it was just the comet. He shrugged unconsciously. He wasn't superstitious, yet his instincts tingled. Still, there was nothing he could put his finger on.

He glanced at the identical house on the opposite side of the street, taking a final drag on the cigarette. Though they'd held the house under constant surveillance for seventy-two hours, and he didn't need to observe the target location again, the comet's incandescent beauty had drawn him outside one more time. The color of its tail was a breathtaking shade of pale green, making the twilight look like a cheap movie—day-for-night photography shot by an inexperienced cameraman. When he'd seen the return of Halley's comet in 1989, he'd been disappointed. Just a faint dot in the night sky. According to the experts, Saracen was an anomaly. Since the start of contemporary records, astronomers had never had the opportunity to observe a comet so close to earth. But they could have a field day with their observations and theories: he had work to do.

Traffic hummed softly in the distance. Lang, the team's surveillance specialist, reported there'd been little movement around the house all day. A member of the Cali cartel and one of the rogue DEA agents had taken a walk around the grounds. Other than that, they stayed inside.

"Security's lax," Lang had stressed when Corvino arrived and they sat down to go over the layout of the house. "They have one guard patrolling the garden every half an hour.

"It's pathetic," he added contemptuously. A former top security analyst for Great Britain's MI5, Lang had advised the SAS on the Iranian hostage siege in London back in the mid-seventies. One of the many jewels in his surveillance and strategy crown. As far as Corvino was concerned, the simpler the better, and if the Cali Cartel were getting cocky, screw 'em.

The face of his Glycine Airman wristwatch showed 08:51 P.M. Corvino ground out the cigarette and entered the bedroom.

Dean Harris lay on the bed staring at the ceiling, chewing gum. The former SEAL commando looked expectantly at Corvino as he entered.

"Ready?" Corvino said, picking up an Ingram MAC-10 nestled in a shoulder holster from the bedside table. Once it was in place, he donned a casual, thin black cotton jacket.

"Is the Pope Catholic?" Harris mouthed through the gum.

Corvino waited for Harris to switch off the bedside lamp before he opened the door connecting the two bedrooms.

Skolomowski, Corvino's back-up, sat in an armchair in the corner quietly sharpening the large blade of his survival knife. Lang sat on a fold-out chair in front of the window, his eyes glued to night vision binoculars standing on a tripod.

"Status?"

"Someone went into the bathroom around ten minutes ago. Five of them in the living room right now. The guard does his rounds on schedule."

"Too easy," muttered the Pole, examining the blade of the knife. "No challenge."

"Jesus, Skolly, what do you want, downtown Beirut?" Harris snapped as he placed four magazines of ammunition in the belt beneath his jacket. "Makes a change to have a simple hit."

Much as he didn't like the Pole because he enjoyed killing, Corvino agreed with Skolomowski. The assignment was insultingly simple for a group like Spiral, Black Ops' crack hit team.

*We could use local talent*, Section Chief Ryan Del Valle had noted to Corvino during the pre-op briefing, *but Hershman insists.*

Corvino had sat without speaking in Del Valle's office. Orders were orders, but he'd silently questioned the necessity of sending top operatives to carry out such a basic mission—execute four members of the Cali Cartel, main suppliers of cocaine to the U.S., and two rogue DEA agents who'd turned, taking with them ten million dollars of unmarked agency bills. Terminate with extreme prejudice, extract the money, and depart.

"Time to move," Corvino said, consulting his watch. It was 8:55.

"Synchronize. Eight fifty-five—"

"And twenty-five seconds," Lang added.

"Check," Harris said.

"Check," said the Pole, sheathing the knife.

"Let's go."

Harris headed for the hallway. Corvino followed.

The stairs creaked as they descended to the first floor. The old house had stood empty for several months until a few days ago when Mitra Alonso, the team's local contact, had leased it from a real estate company in downtown Panama City.

As they reached the door, Harris paused, pulling a silver dollar from his pocket. The coin had a small indentation near the circumference where a .38 bullet had hit during an operation in Boston back in '92. Their target had been an IRA cell whose members were shipping Semtex to Britain. The mission had been one of the few blots on Spiral's almost perfect record; a terrorist had escaped, murdered a bystander on a Cambridge street, and nearly killed Harris, who took a bullet in the shoulder and would have received a second in the chest if the slug hadn't hit his wallet.

Harris held the coin up and kissed it. Corvino smiled faintly at the superstitious act. He found it impossible to believe in anything but himself and his skills as an assassin. There was no God, no Fate, just the ability to kill and survive.

"Finished?"

"Sure." Harris opened the door.

All the houses in the area were set well back from the street, fronted by high walls or a thick screen of trees to insure privacy. As they reached the sidewalk Corvino glanced around casually. To an idle observer, the two men could be friends heading off for a night out at a bar. They strolled across the deserted street, their weapons concealed by their loose jackets.

The Cartel safe house was surrounded by an eight-foot white brick wall, the entrance an ornate iron gate with an electronic lock operated by a manual switch on the other side. They approached the entrance slowly. Harris stopped, removed a pack of Marlboros from his pocket, offered one to Corvino. Playing along with the act, he declined. As Harris lit the cigarette, Corvino scanned the street. *Clear*, he nodded, linking his fingers into a foothold, tossing the cigarette to one side. Corvino lifted and Harris reached the top of the wall, swinging himself over with the grace of an acrobat. Corvino heard his partner drop lightly on the other side of the wall. Within seconds the gate clicked open and Corvino slipped inside.

"If the guard's on schedule, he'll be here in two minutes,' Harris said.

Corvino nodded in the direction of the house.

They broke from the wall's cover, sticking to the patches of shadow cast by the trees. Twilight had slipped into night, a full moon riding low in the sky behind the house, but the strange light of the comet illuminated the front yard. They moved silently across the two hundred yards to a clump of bushes near the front door. Somewhere inside, a radio played, faint strains of classical music leaking from an open upstairs window around the right side of the house. The wall lamp next to the front door was switched off, and the front of the building was shrouded with shadows.

Harris slid a stiletto blade from a sheath on his belt as he blended with the shadows. Corvino removed a silenced 9mm from beneath his jacket, clicking the safety off as he took up a position on the opposite side of the front door.

9:02 P.M.

They waited.

9:05 came and went. Lang had said the guard made his circuit at five and thirty-five past the hour, always walking clockwise around the building.

At 9:10, Corvino shifted slightly, relaxing his shoulder muscles. Where was the guard? Other than the faint echo of music, he could hear no signs of life from inside the house. He knew from the house's floor plan that the main living area was at the rear. He decided to reconnoiter the left side. Signaling his intentions to Harris, Corvino crept silently through the shadows. He paused at the corner, crouching down, and risked a look to confirm the coast was clear. Nothing. Light spilled from a window two hundred feet away. The living room. He slipped around the corner.

When he reached the window, he listened intently. Just the radio or sound system, whatever the music was coming from; Chopin's *Nocturnes*, he now realized.

Angling himself to peer in diagonally through the glass, his face away from the rectangle of light, he froze.

A thick streak of gore decorated a white wall, and a bloody corpse lay beside the couch.

*What the hell?*

He ducked down, adrenaline racing through his body. Positioning himself on the other side of the window, he risked a second look.

The rest of the room was an abattoir. Blood and entrails were strewn across the polished wood floor. A mutilated body he recognized as one of the DEA agents sat slumped in the far corner. Another lay under a mahogany table in a fetal position.

Before he could absorb the details, a cold hand grabbed the back of his neck, slamming his head against the wall.

Corvino's vision exploded into a nebula of white stars.

«« — »»

From Wet Work by Philip Nutman © 2005
Release Date: August 1, 2005 ISBN: 1–892950–67–7

# POWDER

## A.R. Morlan

She still has the vestiges of her peripheral vision left. And with that somewhat blurry outermost sight, she can see Sophie Sunshine's shapeless beige coat, as the old woman scurries from the nurses' station cross the hallway from her hospital bed to other points now beyond her limited peripheral vision to still other spots up and down the narrow slice of shiny-floored hallway outside her room.

She wishes, not for the first time since coming-to here, that she was sicker, even more debilitated, so that she would be now resting — unmoving — in the intensive care wing of the hospital. In the place where Sophie Sunshine's visits would be both limited and monitored; not that being there would stop the old woman, oh no, she knows that she could never be that lucky, but at least someone would be watching her closely, listening to her cloying old-woman words, and (perhaps, although she knows now that such luck will remain forever beyond her now stilled grasp) maybe even catching the subtle meanings behind the plosive syllables issuing from that liver-lipped babbling mouth — before throwing Sophie Sunshine out of the room, for good.

But even when the nurses are hovering around her, picking up her slack arms, wrapping crinkling black blood pressure cuffs around her yielding, still slightly mottled flesh, or poking that temperature taking air-gun into her ear (the eardrum has popped more than once, but the nurses ignore what she at least thinks is the grimace she makes each time they take her temperature), they do not pay attention to Sophie Sunshine's words, or the way she paws and kneads her limp free hand and arm, her husk-dry fingers and slapping-flat palms rubbing, always rubbing, across the flesh Sophie Sunshine herself helped to create, albeit a generation earlier.

The flesh she has longed to touch for all these lonely years, she burbles, always when a sympathetic nurse is there to hear her abandoned old-woman crooning. But, Sophie Sunshine assures the nurses, her voice segueing from self-pity to gloating within the shift from one syllable to another (and never do the nurses catch that shift in tone, or notice how those tears in the old woman's voice so abruptly dry themselves), she won't be lonely any more, not after her little girl is ready to come home from the hospital. For her Grandma, her Baba will be ready and willing to take care of her. And Sophie Sunshine is strong for her age; wasn't she out doing a shuffling, shirt-lifting little dance in the hallway by the nurses' station, half an hour ago, just lifting her feet and swaying her bloat-bellied body out of sheer joy because her darling grand-daughter lived through that terrible accident? That Sophie Sunshine can even find it in herself to smile bravely after her own daughter died in the same accident?

She has heard the nurses talking about Sophie Sunshine, has heard them marveling about how lively and up on things she is for someone in their eighties. Despite Sophie Sunshine's own medical problems (relatively few of them for a woman so old, so ballooned from within with that cyst-like growth in her ovaries that has ridden in her belly like a stillborn fetus for as long as she can remember), they are confident that the old woman will be able to tend to her grown grand-daughter. Not — they whisper just loud enough for her to hear from her silent, flat bed — that Sophie Sunshine will be burdened for all that long…while it's amazing that anyone could've survived in a house so filled with carbon monoxide, none of them think that the grand-daughter will make it over the long haul. Too much lung damage, and all that un-told brain damage…

She still has the last vestiges of her sense of touch left. And with that albeit limited feeling, she knows automatically without needing to open her eyes after shutting them to block out sight of Sophie Sunshine's glistening liver lips, her stained dentures — that the old woman is touching her again. Those dry as old newspapers hands are kneading her exposed arm, before making yet another furtive foray under the thin hospital blanket, to by-pass her waist while groping ever downward the only slightly knobby fingers inching toward the flattened tangle of hair under the scrunched-up gown —

— until the nurse, doesn't matter which one, all of them are so alike in their cheerless smocked sameness, comes into the room, and suddenly Sophie Sunshine's lizard fingers are gone, but as the nurse pokes and wraps and lifts her unprotesting heavy limbs, she knows that the nurse wouldn't have stopped, Sophie Sunshine even if the old woman hadn't pulled her hands out from beneath that flimsy, sterile-smelling blanket. The nurses all adore Sophie Sunshine. She is cheerful, so helpful, so eager to learn all the subtleties of taking care of an invalid, that surely they would forgive her for openly fondling her comatose grandchild.

Sophie Sunshine is blameless. She wasn't at fault when it, came to the accident itself…even though her daughter and grand-daughter wouldn't have been living in that particular house, with that particular defective boiler, if it hadn't been for Sophie Sunshine driving them from the home they'd once shared with her, because of all the things she did to them. Things which occurred out of the sight and hearing of the hospital staff which is so enchanted with the swollen-bodied old woman now.

Sophie Sunshine is just so lonely. Her daughter only saw her once a week, while the grand-daughter (she can hear them whispering about her, as they think she can't hear or understand them) hadn't seen the grandmother who loved her so much in over a decade. Such a long time for an old woman to sit waiting for a word from an ungrateful grandchild.

Some of the workers at the hospital think it is fitting that the grand-daughter will now spend all of her time with Sophie Sunshine; it wasn't fair that such a cheerful, but lonely old woman spend her last years without her own flesh and blood at her side.

She doubts that Sophie Sunshine is interested in the *blood* part, but she knows how the old woman feels about the flesh.

How she loves to feel the flesh. And the workers only voice approval of what Sophie Sunshine is doing. Because she is so active, because she is so funny and lively, always doing, and doing —

She still has a relatively keen sense of smell left. And thanks to that remaining still-intact sense, she knows long before, it happens that one or another of the nurses is coming with the powder. The thick chalky sweetness of it sets fire to her already burning lungs, but the reaction is not one of mere physical pain. Even though she keeps her eyes closed, and tries not to let herself feel the almost weightless smoothness of it as it sprinkles down on her flesh, the smell invoked its own set of stimuli, its own set of memories. And, even worse, sometimes Sophie Sunshine hurries to her side while the nurse is tending to her, making the voice-memories all the more real...

Freshly toweled off from her daily afternoon bath, Baba stands naked in her bedroom in front of her grand-daughter. Her belly — taut, pearlescent in its blue-veined whiteness — rises like a mottled full moon above her already graying tangle of still damp hair down there, and the bottoms of her sagging, pap-like breasts (the side on one breast is marred with a raised white scar, a reminder of The Time Baba Almost Died in the Hospital) almost touch that full-blown globe of a belly. While her grand-daughter holds the can of powder in her tiny hands (even with both hands trying to encircle the rounded corners of the square can, the girl cannot make her fingers or thumbs meet), Baba sits down on the edge of her bed like an empress on her throne, then spreads her legs before telling the girl to put the powder on her hands first, before patting it all over the almost-dry fuzzy hair, and the thin flaps of flesh beneath them.

But Baba is never satisfied with the job the girl does, the powder does not cover enough. Always more powder is needed; Baba's jutting belly shadows the girl's hands as the small fingers go in deeper, into the place with the springy-ringed tube of flesh that goes up and in too far for those tiny fingers to reach.

Only then is Baba satisfied. Just as she is never satisfied when helping her grand-daughter dry herself after her bath until the time when Baba has powdered and probed the even smaller elastic spot down there on her grand-daughter, in the place where no frizzy hair has grown yet.

That tube of elastic flesh has a name — Possible. The girl knows no other name for it, other than what her Baba has told her.

(And always, the powdering and the things that have to do with Possible come only when the mother is away, working, and not there to see or hear.)

But the times of powder and Possible grow fewer as the girl grows her own frizzy hair, and her own chest fills out to hang in saggy blobs of flesh; maybe her fingers are too big for Baba's possible, maybe it is because her fingers and thumbs now meet when holding the can of powder. No reason is given for the end of this after-bath ritual. None is sought. Nothing happened.

But when the girl is no longer a girl, but almost a woman, and the boy lying next to her tells her to feel free, to feel what she wants on him, there is nothing for her to feel. No springy ring of elastic flesh. Only something hard and hanging out, as if

Possible had somehow shoved itself out of the cavern under the shelf-like belly. No matter what it is, or how it got there, it feels like…nothing to her. No more stimulating than grasping an inanimate tube. And there is no smell of powder, only sweat and something more sour. And just as there is nothing for her to feel, what he does to her feels like next to nothing. Numb flesh only going through the emotions.

She remembers the flaps, and what was hidden beyond Possible, and even though she realizes that was wrong, despite the lack of pleasure on her part, what she is doing (trying to do) now is equally numb, equally non-pleasurable. No reason is given by her for ending it before he is through. None is sought. Nothing happened.

She still knows the difference between one set of smoothing, patting hands, and those of another person. And she allows her eyes to open, just a slit obscured by the lashes, when she feels Sophie Sunshine's too-intense hands rubbing her own limp, powered leg. Sophie Sunshine's pendulous belly is still hidden by the old beige coat she's worn ever since her grandchild can remember, and her sagging breasts are likewise covered, but nothing can hide her powdery smell. With each movement of Sophie Sunshine's rubbing arm, the scent wafts off of her, a harshly sweet odor smothering her prone grand-daughter.

(She wishes she had been able to breathe in the odorless poison more freely, to suck it in great lungfulls like her mother had done, until she'd rested completely stiff on the downstairs bed…unable to breathe in either the odorless gas or anything with a more distinctive scent.)

Above her, the nurse is praising Sophie Sunshine. She is a good little nurse, taking such good care of her doll-still grandchild, so eager to do everything right. The nurse promises her that tomorrow, Sophie Sunshine will be shown how to insert the catheter, and how to clean it so that the grand-daughter will not die of some infection. Sophie Sunshine's hands bear down hard on her skin as she tells the nurse that she can't wait, while she kneads the powdery surface of her little girl's flesh.

Sophie Sunshine's eyes are good, and her hands are steady. She will be able to thread in the tube of clear plastic, into that small spot next to Possible, before sprinkling on the powder the nurses will hand to her.

She still has no control over her bladder. And she cannot shift away from Sophie Sunshine's probing fingers, when they keep missing the smaller hole during the first few tries with the catheter. But the nurses keep encouraging Sophie Sunshine to keep trying, assuring her that everything is possible with practice.

They know the old woman will get it right eventually.

«« —»»

From SMOTHERED DOLLS by A.R. Morlan © 2005
Release Date: September 5, 2005 ISBN: 1–892950–71–5

# CARNIVAL

## Christopher Fahy

He took out his costume and spread it across the bed as the strel rushed into his muscles and blood, making him taut and cold. He knelt and felt the costume's smoothness, touched its fur to his lips. It was beautiful, perfect: a jet-black jaguar with claws and teeth of steel. He had worked on the costume for all of six months, and now as he held it, felt its luxury, he filled with pride. His head was funny with strel as he thought: A cat to catch a bird.

Shivering from strel and excitement he took off his clothes, slipped into the costume and zipped it up. He fit the mask carefully over his head and stepped to the full length mirror that hung on the door. Before him stood a lithe and deadly predator, all black except for its claws and fangs and the white and pink of its crotch. In other years, when his goals were different, Haller had filled the sexual border with rich designs that wound around his thighs and spread their colorful tendrils across his chest. This year, the border was a simple gash through which his genitals hung unadorned. This year he was not on the prowl for sex, he was after much bigger game: this year he was out to kill—to kill a bird.

He was positive that Kroll would dress as a bird. For months he'd analyzed Kroll's conversations, watched his every mannerism. Kroll had put crumbs on the windowsill for the sparrows to eat all month. And the number of times he'd referred to flight: his visit to the air museum, the gliding exhibition he'd seen down South. (With Wagner once, he'd even spread his arms to simulate the glider's wings.) Those pensive moments when he smoked and gazed across the city: he was dreaming of flying then, and Haller knew it. Kroll would be a bird for sure, and as Haller looked in the mirror and flexed his claws, he thought: And I am the perfect cat to end that vile bird's life.

His stomach contracted with hunger but he had no desire for food. He went back to the living room, sat on the couch, and listened to the drumming as it came through the open window. The beat was faster now and excited voices—laughter, shouting—rose from the street below. He clipped his strelflask onto his waist-band, then went to the bedroom and took his billyclub out of his bureau drawer.

The billy was new and it was a beauty, longer than the standard model and with slightly more lead in its end. Haller took a few practice swings, tapping the billy's weight against his palm. It was two grams over the limit, but what the hell, they'd never pick him up for a minor infraction like that.

Billyclubs were the only sanctioned weapons during Carnival—but not the only weapons used. While knives had been outlawed years before, the revelers got around the rule by designing costumes with claws and beaks and fangs. As long as a blade was not detachable, it wasn't questioned. Of course, only troopers had guns.

Haller snapped the billyclub onto his waistband, strapped his genital shield to his left wrist, looked in the mirror again. The strel was almost at its peak and his juices surged. He looked at his jaguar head, his gleaming fangs, his vicious claws. He cupped his shield across his genitals and lunged at the mirror with his club. He was ready, ready to kill, and he closed the living room window, turned off the lights, and went through the door.

The moon was high and nearly full, the drums were loud. No shuttles now, no vehicles of any kind, just costumed figures capering in moon-bright dark. A blazing torch threw shattered streaks on painted faces, fur-covered loins, dark glistening pubic hair. Coarse shouts and throaty laughter—and from somewhere nearby, a scream.

Haller turned. Three figures on the corner—a spider, a ghost, and a shark with ragged teeth. They had an old man up against a building and were jabbing at him with their billyclubs, poking his stomach and chest and laughing harshly. The old man whimpered and pleaded and swore that he had no money, which only made the revelers prod him more. Young punks and their kid games, Haller thought. They hadn't learned to focus yet, to use the Carnival. Well, most never did, fools that they were. He watched the old man whine and cringe as the clubs came down. He felt a twinge of pity, but after all, the man had only himself to blame for his plight. If he'd missed evacuation, the least he could have done was stay inside. It was no guarantee of safety, God only knew, but to be old and on the streets in Carnival time, you had better be ready to die.

The shark brought his billy down again, and again the old man screamed. The ghost and spider laughed. Haller would have routed the punks in other years, but this year he had a mission, and to risk an injury to save an old man's life would be insane.

The street held dozens of revelers now. He joined them and started toward Center Square. From every direction they came, each doing the up-and-down Carnival dance to the pulse of the drums. Soon the street was a river of beasts: tigers, leopards, bears and lions, panthers, zebras, wolves. There were monsters and gargoyles, gnomes and fairies, goblins and witches and trolls. There were birds—many birds: bright-feathered cockatoos, peacocks and parrots; dun-colored hawks and coal-black crows. There were fantasy birds, birds hatched in imaginations feral and dark, but none was the bird Haller sought.

The crowd thickened and swelled, and Haller was locked in its pulsating center, shield across his genitals, his right paw high in the air. The drumming grew louder, the dancing turned wild, the strel was icy fire in Haller's veins. He banged up hard against a buffalo that snarled and faked a swing with its billy, but Haller snarled back and cocked his paw and the buffalo bowed and laughed.

The crowd closed in and Haller was jammed against hot flesh. A bird of paradise strutted against him, rubbing her naked buttocks against his crotch. He didn't want it, didn't want to get caught up in it, he tried to back away but was once again squeezed against slippery flesh. He fought his primal urge—then desperately, impulsively, he freed his hand from his steel-tipped paw and slipped two fingers between the wild bird's legs.

For a second her dancing stopped: then it started again and she shrieked with excitement and Haller could feel her quivering wet on his hand. He thrust deeper, making her moan. Then the crowd surged forward, wrenching her out of his reach, and he stumbled, caught himself, was struck on the jaw by a flying elbow, and soon his erection was gone.

Far away in the back of his head, behind the drums, the choo-choo scream of chuffa-whistles, Haller cursed himself. He'd promised himself to avoid distractions and already had succumbed. He had to stay centered, keep his focus clear: only by doing that could he succeed.

The river of flesh moved steadily forward; at last it reached Center Square. Haller was wedged against pulsating bodies that stretched for blocks, stretched as far as the eye could see. On Tuesday he_d eaten his lunch in this very square, had placidly watched dull pigeons peck crusts of bread, watched women with bulging shopping bags sink wearily onto the benches to catch their breath. Now most of those women were far from here, the pigeons were roosting high up on the ledges of buildings, and Center Square was a dazzling explosion of feathers and fur and sweat and paint and steel. The drumbeats battered Haller's thoughts, buzzed in his breastbone, rattled his jaw and skull. On the lampposts the torches flickered and pulsed, throwing lightning across the grotesques. Paws thrust toward the silver moon, claws flashed. The crowd surged one way, then another, gaps opened and closed.

A tug at his waistband: quickly he whirled, shielding his crotch, lashing out with his claws. The thief jumped sideways, clutching its chest. A monkey, short and slim, and it screamed, "A taste, you bastard! That's all I wanted, a taste!" It staggered, its fur stained red. Raising his billyclub, Haller shouted, "I'll break your goddamn skull!" The monkey stumbled backward and disappeared.

The combat, brief though it was, had taken its toll. Haller was shivery, cold, his arms felt weak. The first rush of strel had died, and thin sharp pangs of hunger cramped his gut.

It took him almost half an hour to fight his way to the edge of the square, another half hour to get to where the crowd was sparse enough to allow him to move unhampered. By then he was tired. Out only two hours and already tired. He couldn't afford to be tired so soon. He needed food; some food and he'd be all right.

The tavern reeked of smoke and alcohol. It was chaos, the end of the counter awash with beer and wet chunks of food. Paws snatched and clutched, mouths sucked and chewed. During Carnival, food and drink were free—except for strel, of course—and anyone who ran short of strel would have to wait hours for more.

Haller grabbed a turkey leg from a steaming bowl. As he did, a hand closed over his crotch. A Siamese cat with pointed breasts and golden pubic hair. She stroked his organs. He pulled away. "Doesn't the big pussycat want to play?" she purred, and in spite of himself, he grew firm. "That's so much better," the Siamese said, and lowered her mouth to his groin. He jerked back sharply, his heart pounding hard in his head.

Near the wall, he devoured the turkey, swallowing meat in big chunks. Revelers shouted, gorged themselves, and grabbed each others' genitals. Haller's mouth was dry: when he swallowed, the meat felt like stone. He finished it, went back to the counter and grabbed a mug of beer. The cat was gone. He drank enough beer to quench his thirst and thought of Kroll. He took a sip from his strelflask, went back to the street.

A rhinoceros was relieving himself beside the tavern door; the urine splashed on the wall in a hard thick stream. On the pavement below lay the Siamese, her legs embracing the waist of a husky lion. The lion's naked flanks thrust into her; she gasped and groaned. Haller quickly turned into the street and thought of Kroll. That was all he would think of, Kroll.

Again he was carried along on the throbbing sea. Apparitions flashed before him, disappeared. A scuffle ahead and the monsters scattered. Two helmeted troopers, shiny and black, cracked their clubs on a vulture's skull. Haller watched as they dragged the bird off. It was some other vulture, not Kroll. He drank more strel.

For more than two hours he chanted and pranced and shrieked. The moon reached its zenith and started to fall, the air turned strangely warm. Hollow eyes swam in front of him; swollen mouths cackled and spit. Fangs, claws and beaks flashed past, flesh pressed his flesh. He shouted the chant at the top of his lungs, he pounded his feet on the pavement hard, he beat on the back of the creature in front as the creature behind beat him. It felt good, so good after such a long time—but not as good as in other years, because he was holding back, he was saving himself for the job he must do, the job he had to this year or not at all.

«« — »»

*Carnival* a short story in MATINEE AT THE FLAME by Christopher Fahy ©
2005
Release Date: October 3, 2005 ISBN: 1–892950–73–1

# THE TERY

## F. Paul Wilson

### PROLOGUE

As they approached the crude stone chapel, the priest's hopes became a subvocal litany – *A whole planetful of Christians . . . too good to be true . . . bound to be disappointed* – running through his head in a reverberating circuit until it blurred all other thoughts. But its inherent defeatism could not damp the tingling anticipation charging through him.

The planet had been opened only recently to outside contact and trade. Its original settlers had cut themselves off from the rest of humanity many centuries ago. But their descendents – most of them, anyway – had different ideas.

The present population was divided into two nations. The smaller island country – inhabited, it was said, by "Talents," or something like that – wanted nothing to do with the Fed and so was to be left alone. The larger nation, however, welcomed the chance to rejoin the mainstream of interstellar humanity, and it was this segment of the population that interested Gebi Pirella, S.J.

His mission was one of critical importance to the Amalgamated Church of Unified Christendom because the inhabitants here had been described as followers of a distinctly Christian-like religion, complete with crucifixes. Early trade envoys who had been permitted a brief glance inside one of the chapels mentioned that the crucifixes were somehow *different*, but gave no specifics.

No matter. News of the existence of a planet-wide Christian enclave would prove incalculably important to the stagnating Unified Church, spreading its name and hopefully drawing converts from all over Occupied Space.

"The cross is just a symbol, of course," Mantha was saying as he pointed to the top of the chapel. He was a big, fair-haired man wearing only a loincloth in the heat. His grammar and speech pattern carried an archaic ring. "Not an object of worship. We revere the one who died upon it and hold to the lesson of brotherhood he taught us."

Father Pirella nodded. "Of course"

Heartening to know, and the first exposition of faith he had been able to wrest from this taciturn native who seemed to serve as some sort of ecclesiastical administrator to the locale.

The Jesuit had pushed their initial conversation toward a discussion of theological concepts but soon discovered that he and Mantha did not share the same vocabulary on religious matters. Beyond determining that the religious sect in question was less than two centuries old – unsettling, that, but surely not without a satisfactory explanation – Father Pirella's most basic questions had been met with an uncomprehending stare. He had suggested that the easiest and most logical solution was to go to the nearest structure and start there with concrete articles. After establishing a little common ground, they could then progress to abstractions.

Mantha had agreed.

The native held the door open for him – hinges…the technological level here was startlingly depressed – and Father Pirella entered the cool dim interior.

He saw seats but no altar. Stark and alone, a huge, life-size crucifix dominated the far end of the chamber. He hurried forward, eager to study it. Merely to find the Christ figure here on this isolated world would be quite enough; but to demonstrate that it held a central position in the culture would be more than anyone in the order or the Church had ever dreamed. It would be the consummation of –

*"Mother of God!"*

The words echoed briefly in the dimness. Father Pirella's feet began to slide on the polished floor as he recoiled in horror at the sight of the figure on the cross. Crushing disappointment fanned his indignation.

"This is sacrilege!" he hissed through clenched teeth framed in tight, bloodless lips. *"Blasphemy!"*

For a moment he almost gave in to the urge to hurl himself at the astonished and confused Mantha, then he shuddered and rushed out into the bright, wholesome daylight.

"I did not know what you were looking for," Mantha said when he finally caught up to Father Pirella, "but I had a feeling you would not find it in there."

"Why didn't you warn me?"

Mantha gently took the priest's arm and began to lead him down a path through the trees.

"Come. Come with me to God's-Touch and you will perhaps understand."

Father Pirella allowed himself to be led. God's-Touch? What was that? It certainly couldn't be any worse than what he had just seen.

"Everything starts a long time ago," Mantha was saying. "One hundred and sixty-seven of our years, to be exact. It begins in a field not too far from here…"

### -I-

They hadn't left him for dead. They had to know he was still alive, had to see the shallow expansion and contraction of his blood-smeared rib cage as he lay on his face in the grass. But they had other stops to make and he took such a long time dying. A tery didn't merit a final stroke to end it all, so they left him to the scavengers.

Consciousness ebbed and flowed, and every time he opened his eyes he found the world filled with flies and gnats. He tried but could not lift his arms to brush them away. Each time he tried, the effort involved dropped him again into oblivion. Which wasn't a bad place to be. Dark and quiet, no pain there.

But he always came back. Soon, if he was lucky, he would remain sunken there forever. Why not stay there? Everyone who meant anything to him had been taken away.

The creak of a poorly lubricated wooden axle pulled him to consciousness again. He heard stealthy footsteps through the ground against his left ear and allowed himself to hope.

Maybe another tery…

Summoning whatever reserve was left in his body, he pushed against the ground with his right arm and tried to roll over. The daylight suddenly dimmed and he knew he was losing consciousness, but he held on and managed to get a little leverage from his left arm, which had been pinned under him. He moved. A shift in his shoulder girdle and suddenly he was rolling onto his back amid a cloud of angry flies.

The effort cost him another period of awareness. When he came to again, the creaking was gone. Despair crushed him. The furtiveness of the footsteps he had heard was proof enough that they belonged to another tery, for stealth simply was not the way of the human soldiers who trampled everything in their path. Now the footsteps were gone and with them his last hope of rescue.

He was dying and knew it. If the hot, drying sun and his festering wounds didn't kill him by nightfall, one of the big nocturnal predators would finish the task. He couldn't decide which he –

Footsteps again…

The same ones, light and stealthy, but much closer now. The passing creature must have seen some movement in the tall grass and come over to investigate. It had probably crouched at a cautious distance and watched.

The tery lay still and hoped. He could do no more.

The footsteps stopped by his head and a face looked down at him. A human face, bearded, with bright blue eyes. He lost all hope then. If he could have found his voice he would have screamed in anguish, frustration, and despair.

But the human neither ignored him nor further mistreated him. Instead, he squatted and inspected the near countless lacerations that covered his body. His face grew dark with…could it be anger? The tery was not adept at reading human expressions. The man muttered something unintelligible as his inspection progressed.

Shaking his head, the human rose and moved around to a position behind the tery's head. He bent and hooked a hand under each of the tery's arms, then tried to lift him. It didn't work. The human lacked the strength to move his considerable weight, and the slight change in position sent a white-hot jolt of pain through each wound. The tery wanted to scream at him to stop, but all he could manage was a low, agonized moan.

The human loosened his grip and stood up, apparently uncertain of this next step.

"Can you speak?" the man said.

The odd question startled the tery. Yes, he could speak. He tried but his tongue was too thick and dry and swollen for a single word.

"Can you understand?"

The tery closed his eyes. Why the questions? What did it matter, anyway? He was going to die here. Why didn't this strange human just go away and leave him in peace?

After a brief pause, the man tore a strip of cloth from the coarse shirt he wore and laid it over the tery's eyes. Then he strolled away. The sound of his retreating footsteps was soon joined by the creak of the wooden axle. Both eventually faded beyond perception.

It was a small act of kindness, that strip of cloth, and incomprehensible to the tery. Why a human should want to keep the flies off his eyes while the rest of him died was beyond him, but he appreciated the comfort it offered.

The sun blazed on him and he felt his tongue grow thicker and drier during the progressively shorter periods of consciousness. Soon one of those periods would be his last.

He was brought to again by minute vibrations in the ground at the back of his head. Trotting hooves, and something dragging. The soldiers were returning. He was almost glad. Perhaps they would trample him as they passed and quickly end it all.

But the hoofbeats stopped and footsteps approached – many feet. The cloth was pulled from his eyes with an abrupt motion and the faces that leaned over him were human but didn't belong to soldiers. The four of them glanced at each other and nodded silently. One with blond hair turned and moved from view while the others, much to the tery's surprise, bent over him and began to brush the flies and gnats from his wounds. All this without a single word.

The blond man returned with one of the mounts. From a harness around its neck, a long pole ran along each shaggy flank to end on the ground well beyond the hindquarters. Rope was basket-woven between the poles.

Still no word was spoken.

Their silence puzzled him, for they were obviously on their guard. What was there to fear in these woods besides Kitru's troops? And what had these humans to fear from Kitru, who slew only teries?

The appearance of a water jug halted further speculation. Its mouth was placed against his lips and a few drops allowed to trickle out. The tery tried to gulp but succeeded only in aspirating a few drops, which started him coughing. The jug was withdrawn, but at least his tongue no longer felt like dried leather.

With the utmost gentleness and an uncanny coordination of effort, the four men lifted the tery. The pain came again, but not as bad a when the first one had tried to lift him. They carried him and placed him across the webbing of the drag, then tied him down with cloth strips. All without speaking.

Perhaps they were outlaws. But even so, the tery began to think them overly cautious in their silence. The soldiers were long gone.

The humans mounted and ambled their steeds toward the deep forest. The uneven ground jostled the drag and caused a few of his barely clotted wounds to reopen, but the tery bore the pain in silence. He felt safe and secure, as if everything was going to be all right. And he hadn't the vaguest notion why he should feel that way.

«≪—≫»

From THE TERY by F. Paul Wilson © 1989, 2005
Release Date: October 3, 2005 ISBN: 1–892950–32–4

# THE JADE UNICORN
## Jay Halpern

—There are no energies greater than those of terror, agony, and despair, said Mercadante to the Master.

They stood in the catacombs beneath the Chateau, Mercadante dwarfed by his pupil. The Master's shaggy presence filled the dark, rat-infested tunnels with a hideous stench and his guttural breathing echoed in a thousand reverberations. But to Mercadante the sound of this breathing was the cadence of freedom, and the stench the fragrance of dominion and power.

He filled his lungs unrestrainedly with the tainted air as he spoke.

— This castle has known innumerable victims to the lusts of its owners in the hundreds of years since it was built. Their corpses have all been brought down here for disposal. You see lining the stone walls of these catacombs the skulls and bones of these victims: row upon row of grinning death's heads, their vacant eyes now inhabited by rats and other vermin.

Mercadante paused while they both listened to the scratches and scrapes emitted by the rows of countless skulls, an intensity of living sound which had abrogated the wonted silence of the tomb.

— The blood of generations has soaked into this soil. Generations of people in pain and torment. The red fingers of blood which reach down into the earth from here bear with them psychic energies equal to a thousand flaming suns. And I have brought with me casks of earth of even greater potency.

A large iron trunk rested beside a wall of skulls. Mercadante unlocked it and withdrew a small silver casket. The casket was filled with earth.

—The soil of Auschwitz, he said, sprinkling the earth on the ground at the Master's feet.

The Master quivered with a sudden influx of energy.

—The soil of Belsen, the soil of Dachau, the soil of Treblinka…

Mercadante continued opening casket after casket, pouring the earth at his pupil's feet. The soil from great battlefields, from sites of particularly heinous murders: the soils of Hiroshima and Nagasaki and My Lai. Again and again the raw earth settled in clumps at the Master's feet and with each addition the creature moaned orgasmically, its eyes blazing ever brighter, sucking into itself the megaton energies, quivering with the delight of power, growing larger, heavier, more massive and forbidding.

—Open Yourself more fully to these energies, said Mercadante as he began to rapidly chant the litany of infamous names. To all this blazing energy You are heir and successor. Feed on these bloody and stained soils. Take from the earth that which she strives to keep hidden, that which she strives to mourn in silence and secrecy. You have ravished her and all that is hers is now Yours. Feed, O Great One, upon these my offerings of mankind's heritage.

The beast writhed deliciously with the waves of energy that quivered through it. And then, as the clumps of soil mounted at his feet in rhythm with its mentor's dark chant, its mind blossomed with fearsome force and its skull opened like a glass dome to the torchlight and the scuffling vermin and the walls of skulls.

It was then that the wondering Beast witnessed the rising of the ghosts.

Vague, billowing transparencies at first, like the shadows of chimney smoke on a wall. Then the slender forms and faces, rising up from the mound of earth at the Beast's feet, wailing, agonized faces howling their misfortunes to the stars. Some held forth their severed limbs and heads in macabre bundles, some were content to recite the atrocities that had claimed them, some weeped more for loved ones risen in horror by their side than for themselves. A million voices murmuring, weeping, howling at once as wraith upon wraith rose like vapors into the light of the Master's mind.

At last the Beast grew dizzy with the horror, dizzy with the maddening influx of human misery that it sucked from the bloody clumps of earth into the very essence of its being and energy. It howled its triumph and exultation in a massive, trumpeting wail that sprawled Mercadante flat upon the ground, his hands tightly pressed against his ears, his face contorted in pain.

Far above the catacombs, in the Great Hall, the celebrants grew silent and trembled, fearing the rumbling in the earth.

«« —»»

From THE JADE UNICORN by Jay Halpern © 2004
Now Available ISBN: 1-892950-66-9

# RESURRECTION INC.

## TENTH ANNIVERSARY EDITION

## KEVIN J. ANDERSON

| | | |
|---|---|---|
| • Hard Cover | ISBN: 1-892950-07-3 | $45.00 |
| • Sterling 1/100 | ISBN: 1-892950-06-5 | $85.00 |
| • Lettered/Leather 1/26 | ISBN: 1-892950-05-7 | $350.00 |

### INTRODUCTIONS BY
### JANET BERLINER, DAVID B. SILVA & BENTLEY LITTLE

## ORIGINAL COVER ART BY BOB EGGLETON

- **Nominated for Best Novel by the Horror Writer's Association**
- **First Hardcover Edition!!**

Resurrection. Inc. found a profitable way to do it. A microprocessor brain, synthetic heart and blood-presto, anyone with the price could buy a Servant with no mind of it's own, no memories of its past life, and trained to obey any command. But for every Servant created, a living worker was out of a job. Some people took to rioting in the streets, their rampages ruthlessly ended by armored and heavily armed Enforcers, eager for the kill. Some joined the ever-growing cult of neo-Satanism, seeking heaven in the depths of Hell.

Then came Danal. He was dead-murdered in a neo-Satanist sacrifice—but as a Servant he began to remember. Danal learned who had killed him...and what Resurrection, Inc. had in mind for the human race...

Kevin Anderson's first novel Resurrection Inc. was orginally released in paperback only in a short print run. It has not been available again until now. Brought to you with special introductions by guest authors (see above) and with original cover art by World Fantasy Award Winning artist Bob Eggleton. This is also the novels first appearance in hardcover.

 **OVERLOOK CONNECTION PRESS**
PO Box 1934 • Hiram, GA • 30141
PHONE: 678-567-9777 • FAX: 770-222-6192
EMAIL: overlookcn@aol.com
www.overlookconnection.com

# HORROR PLUM'D:
## AN INTERNATIONAL STEPHEN KING BIBLIOGRAPHY AND GUIDE - 1960-2000
### by Michael R. Collings

| | | |
|---|---|---|
| First Edition Trade Paperback | ISBN 1892950316 | $39.95 |
| First Hardcover Edition | ISBN 1892950456 | $59.95 |
| Casebound Library Hardcover | ISBN 1892950308 | $74.95 |

Mr. Collings, author of previous OCP titles Hauntings: Official Peter Straub Bibliography and Storyteller: Official Guide to Orson Scott Card" has brought together you this incredible collection of every book, story, and ephemera published on Stephen King. Including: Books, Novels, Short-Fiction Collections, Non-Fiction, Etc. Including Reprints and multimedia adaptations of book titles. Short Fiction, Screenplays, Anthologies, Audio and Video adaptations, etc. This volume, coming in at almost 600 pages, also features many reproductions of novels from the US and Foreign editions. Almost 100 cover and art reproductions. Thousands of listings that took Mr. Collings over fifteen years to collect. This is a one-of-a-kind volume, and invaluable to any King reader and / or collector to discover the many volumes and listings of and about Stephen King.

CHAPTERS FEATURED IN THE BIBLIOGRAPHY
Σ Bibliography: Book-Length Publications: Fiction, Poetry, Plays
• Short Fictions: Short Stories, Novella
• Unpublished manuscripts
• Non-Fiction: Science Fiction Criticism, Theoretical Essays, and Reviews.
• Video and Audio Tape Dramatic Presentations
• Selected Secondary Sources: Interviews, Reviews, Articles, Biographical sketches, etc.
• This bibliography is Indexed.
• ALSO: Cover art of most novels and collections, rare publications, reproduced here
• Cover Art by Erik Wilson

ABOUT THE AUTHOR: Michael R. Collings is professor of English, director of Creative Writing, and Poet-in-Residence 1997 - 2003 at Pepperdine University, Malibu, California. He has written volumes of poetry; published scholarly and academic studies of authors such as Stephen King, Orson Scott Card, Dean Koontz, and Piers Anthony; and compiled a number of bibliographies.

# OFF SEASON
## THE UNEXPURGATED EDITION
### BY JACK KETCHUM

| | | |
|---|---|---|
| • Trade Limited: | ISBN: 1-892950-10-3 | Sold Out |
| • Trade Hardcover | ISBN: 1-892950-55-3 | $34.95 |
| • Trade Paperback | ISBN: 1-892950-20-0 | $22.95 |

**TRADE LIMITED: 1/1000 - DISTINCTIVE BINDING. ORIGINAL COVER ART BY NEAL McPHEETERS. SIGNED.**

- **INTRODUCTION BY DOUGLAS E. WINTER**
- **AFTERWORD BY JACK KETCHUM**

*"Only a novel of expert articulation and emotional truth can cast such a long shadow, and Ketchum's is both"*
—Publisher's Weekly

When Off Season was first released in 1980, it took readers by storm and sold over 250,000 copies! However, the original edition was edited and content was removed from the story at the publisher's request. The whole effect of the book was deemed too intense, in particular the ending—which is completely restored in this edition. The Overlook Connection Press has released this edition in it's original unexpurgated state for the first time anywhere. Not only is this the author's original vision, but it is also the first world hard cover release. This book has not been available in the US for almost two decades in any edition.

We have a special introduction by Douglas E. Winter, who has championed this novel for years. Also an Afterword by the author Jack Ketchum. Original cover art by Neal McPheeters (cover artist for The Girl Next Door, Red, and Right To Life).

**OVERLOOK CONNECTION PRESS**
PO Box 1934 • HIRAM, GA • 30141
PHONE: 678-567-9777 • FAX: 770-222-6192
EMAIL: overlookcn@aol.com
www.overlookconnection.com

# Red

## BY BRITISH FANTASY AWARD WINNER

## Jack Ketchum

- Signed Hard Cover — ISBN: 1-892950-47-2 — $39.95
- Signed Sterling 1/100 — $85.00
- Signed Lettered/Leather 1/26 — $300.00

## ORIGINAL COVER ART BY NEAL McPHEETERS

JACK KETCHUM

*"…intelligent and real and deeply felt…"*
—Ed Gorman, Cemetery Dance

*"Once again Ketchum tells a gripping tale the way only he can…Avery is probably the most carefully rendered character I've encountered in (his) fiction…Ketchum is a true American original."*
—Hank Wagner, DarkEcho

*"…Ketchum's work is one of the consistant pleasures of contemporary horror/suspense…do yourself a favor and give his tough, compassionate new novel a try…transcends what could have been a standard revenge story and becomes something subtler and more eloquent: a vision of our place in the community of living things."*
—Bill Sheehan,
Overlook Connection Reviews

The old man hears them before he sees them, the three boys coming over the hill, disturbing the peace by the river where he's fishing. He smells gun oil too, too much oil on a brand-new shotgun. These aren't hunters, they're rich kids who don't care about the river and the fish and the old man.

Or his dog.

Red is the name of the old man's dog, his best friend in the world. And when the boys shoot the dog —for nothing, for simple spite—he sees red, like a mist before his eyes.

And before the whole thing is done there'll be more red. Red for blood…

## OVERLOOK CONNECTION PRESS
PO Box 1934 • Hiram, GA • 30141
PHONE: 678-567-9777 • FAX: 770-222-6192
EMAIL: overlookcn@aol.com
www.overlookconnection.com

# GOON

## by Edward Lee & John Pelan

- Author's Preferred Version
- Original cover art by Erik Wilson
- Seven Original/Graphic Interior Illustrations by Micah Hayes.
- Signed Limited Edition Hardcover 1/500 red titles
  $44.95
- HARD COVER: ISBN 1-892950-62-6—yellow titles
  $39.95
- 1/26 Lettered FULL GRAIN Leather edition in wood box. SIGNED by both Authors         $275.00

Six-foot-nine and four hundred pounds, hailing from parts unknown, he is the one-man walking gore-machine of the Deep South Wrestling Conference, and his name is...

### GOON

But police captain Philip Straker isn't a wrestling fan. The bodies pile up like dirty laundry: sex-obsessed tramps used as playthings by some unspeakable creature. Is it just a coincidence, or do all the victims have something in common?

### GOON

Investigative reporter Melinda Pierce will do anything to find out, by offering herself up as a sexual spittoon in order to infiltrate the arcane and lust-drenched warrens of backstage wrestling. She partakes in carnal forays so gross, so downright nasty, they'd make Linda Lovelace bend over and puke. All to track down...

### GOON

Is Goon just a wrestler gone insane? Or is he something hideously worse? Relentless as a Texas Deathmatch, GOON is a no-holds-barred festival of body slams and insatiable orgy, of pile-drivers and sexual grotesquerie, of neck-breakers, drop-kicks and more blood and guts than a fish market floor. It just might leave you down for the count...

The notorious long-sold-out classic of modern horror is back! The Overlook Connection is proud to present this newly illustrated and one of the most talked about—and outrageous—tales to ever be penned in the horror genre.

*"A raunchy riot of rasslin', ringrats, and no-holds-barred sex. A must for fans of over-the-top action and outrageous thrills."*
—Lucy Taylor, author of *The Safety of Unknown Cities* and *The Silence Between The Screams*

## OVERLOOK CONNECTION PRESS
PO Box 1934 • Hiram, GA • 30141
PHONE: 678-567-9777 • FAX: 770-222-6192
EMAIL: overlookcn@aol.com
www.overlookconnection.com

# MIRROR ME

## BY YVONNE NAVARRO

| Signed Limited Edition – Signed by the author | $44.95 |
|---|---|
| First Trade Hardcover  ISBN: 1892950693 | $37.95 |

Mirror Me is Yvonne Navarro's long awaited new novel of horror. This novel begins in the past and takes you to the present day, where a young woman's life is affected in drastic measures.

Hannah Danior is a young woman struggling to build a life after an unspeakable experience in her childhood.  Now self-sufficient, she is nonetheless still tormented by her past... and the cruel demons of her childhood are not finished with her. At any instant and with no warning, she will inexplicably manifest the injuries of someone she's never even met.  Enduring everything from mere bruises to mortal blows, many of her wounds would kill a normal woman, but just as inexplicably, she heals– at astonishing speed– presumably so she can be victimized again.

With her face and body disfigured by countless scars, Hannah desires only to be left alone.  But fate has other ideas when a pair of detectives catch the similarity between her most recent horrific event– where her throat is suddenly cut- - and the murder of a neighborhood woman.  One demands answers she doesn't have and the other, a man she doesn't recognize at all, raises instinctive alarms inside Hannah's head.  When the unthinkable happens and one of the detectives falls in love with her, the search for the truth about Hannah's past and an unseen killer twists itself from the realm of the supernatural into the unforgiving streets of Chicago...

Original cover art by Rick Sardinha.
Limited Edition features unique cover graphics only found on this edition.

## OVERLOOK CONNECTION PRESS
**PO Box 1934 • Hiram, GA • 30141**
**PHONE: 678-567-9777 • FAX: 770-222-6192**
**EMAIL: overlookcn@aol.com**
**www.overlookconnection.com**

The Greyhound pulled into Carruthers, Texas a little after nine and unloaded seventeen people into the unseasonably cold autumn night. All had family waiting for them.

All, except for two.

The Town of Carruthers, Texas, has seen its share of drifters and lowlifes. But never anyone like Steven and Earl...

They move from town to town. Hustling the pool halls. Raising a little hell. Drinking a little blood. They sleep by day and hunt by night—the ultimate predators. The perfect life. Until now.

A barroom brawl ends in disaster. The soil from Steven's grave has been stolen. And a young boy's death sparks an all out war between vampires and mortals that will turn the local Frontier Day celebration into a blood bath...

"Gary's vampires...failed to read the book on how vampires are to behave. They may be less than human, but their actions are very human... And they're disturbing and scary because they're funny... Gary is one of the few writers I've ever read that realizes humor and horror are truly opposite sides of a double edged knife."
—Joe R. Lansdale

"I LOVED IT! It's funny and terrifying, and I couldn't stop reading it!" —Kevin J. Anderson, N.Y. Times bestselling author of Dune: House Atriedes

"Gary Raisor's Less Than Human is a good chunk of a damn fine novel. The author's got an effective voice for capturing the distinctive flavors of the Texas/ Southwestern backdrop for this supernatural thriller. Less Than Human is colorfully inventive, paced at a gallop, and frequently nicely skewed."—Edward Bryant, Locus

"An untraditional setting, a novel look at the undead and their nature, all leavened with some original and very bizarre humor."
—Don D'Ammassa, Science Fiction Chronicle

# Spares
## Michael Marshall Smith

### SIGNED BY ALL CONTRIBUTORS!

- Signed Limited       ISBN: 0-9633397-6-1   $45.00
- Signed Sterling 1/ 100   ISBN: 0-9633397-5-3   $85.00
- Signed Lettered/Leather 1/52   ISBN: 0-9633397-7-X   $400.00

## INTRODUCTION BY NEIL GAIMAN

## ORIGINAL COVER ART BY ALAN M. CLARK

*"...one knows one is in safe hands with Michael Marshall Smith, even if there is dried blood on his fingers, and grave-dirt beneath his fingernails."*
—Neil Gaiman

**Luck?** Don't talk to Jack Randall about luck. He didn't keep up the payment on his, and it ran out a long time ago. The good fortune box is empty. A loner veteran of a savage war, he's spent the last five years buried deep, hiding out on a Spares farm with people who can't even spell luck. Forced to flee this lost bolt-hole, Jack returns to the city that used to be his home. All he wants is to score a little money and disappear with the people he's trying to save. Unfortunately, he's got a talent for attracting trouble—the kind most people would run screaming from. Jack Randall isn't most people. That's part of his problem. His escape from the Farm with six of its inmates (well, five and a half) brings

him head to head with the man who destroyed everything he once held dear.

**He has to make a decision: take revenge or turn away?**

**Michael Marshall Smith** is one of today's most unique and talented young writers. Three times winner of the British Fantasy Award for short fiction—and winner of the August Derleth Award for Best Novel, *Only Forward*. You can find it all right here —Dark Tragi-Comedy-Horror-Future-Thriller—in **SPARES**. Here's an opportunity to own a truly unique volume, **SPARES: THE SPECIAL EDITION.**

- **SPARES: Lost First Chapter**—appears here for the first time anywhere!
- **Three stories that feature elements from this novel:**
  - **The Gap**
  - **Dying**
  - **To Receive is Better**
- **Afterwords by Michael Marshall Smith**

# THE LOST WORKS OF STEPHEN KING

## STEPHEN J. SPIGNESI

### A GUIDE TO UNPUBLISHED MANUSCRIPTS, STORY FRAGMENTS, ALTERNATIVE VERSIONS, & ODDITIES

=LETTERED LEATHER edition. Only 52 copies. Bound in a blue leather, foil embossing artwork front and back, bound in book mark, and a hardwood slipcase with windows. Signed by Stephen Spignesi, Tyson Blue, and James Cole. $350.00

=LIMITED LEATHER edition 1,000 copies. Bound in red leather with gold foil embossing artwork, front and back. Signed by Stephen Spignesi, Tyson Blue, and James Cole. $60.00

## 100 PAGES LONGER THAN THE TRADE EDITION!

- The OCP edition feature pieces ONLY available in this limited
- Twenty pages of photos, many ONLY available in this limited
- "The Irish King" piece ONLY available in this limited edition
- "My Say" by Stephen King rare and reprinted in its entirety

Seventy-five of rarities, twenty newly discovered King pieces discussed here for the first time anywhere, are discussed in detail in *The Lost Work of Stephen King*, providing fascinating insight into King's evolution as a writer and offering the fan a glimpse of hidden wonders he or she will likely never have a chance to learn about any other way. A definition and comprehensive summary of the piece is provided, along with selected excerpts and suggestions as to how to find a copy of the complete work (if one is available).

In addition to this massive amount of material about the Lost Works, the book also includes a lengthy section called "The Royal Library." This feature consists of informative reviews of all of King's mainstream material.

## OVERLOOK CONNECTION PRESS
PO BOX 1934 • HIRAM, GA • 30141
PHONE: 678-567-9777 • FAX: 770-222-6192
EMAIL: overlookcn@aol.com
www.overlookconnection.com

# The Shape Under The Sheet
# The Official Stephen King Encyclopedia
## By Stephen J. Spignesi

**1/350 Signed, Numbered, Slipcased**
**ISBN 1892950111    $175.00**

 **OVERLOOK CONNECTION PRESS**
PO Box 1934 • Hiram, GA • 30141
PHONE: 678-567-9777 • FAX: 770-222-6192
EMAIL: overlookcn@aol.com
www.overlookconnection.com

# THE SILENCE BETWEEN THE SCREAMS

### BY LUCY TAYLOR

*The Silence Between the Screams* features cover art by Rick Sardinha.

**First Edition Hard Cover**
**ISBN 1892950642 $39.95**

A *Silence Between The Screams* is a collection of original short fiction that also features the previously released novella "Spree" which hasn't been available for years. Now "Spree" and this collection of original short fiction has been published together for the first time. *The Silence Between The Screams*, the title story, takes us on a ride with a family that soon discovers that the fabric that makes up our world is not as sound as once thought. That revenge comes in all shapes and sizes in "A Hairy Chest, A Big Dick, and a Harley." Between survival and sacrifice the decisions are decided in "Hymns to Old Gods," and, well, you'll just have to read what this Bram Stoker Award-Winning author, Lucy Taylor, has in store for you.

Also published as a signed limited under the title *A Hairy Chest, A Big Dick, and A Harley* also featuring original cover art by Rick Sardinha. The text is the same, however the limited has many extra features, and interior art.

 **OVERLOOK CONNECTION PRESS**
PO Box 1934 • HIRAM, GA • 30141
PHONE: 678-567-9777 • FAX: 770-222-6192
EMAIL: overlookcn@aol.com
www.overlookconnection.com

# SPECIALTY BOOKSTORES

Please support these stores for any OCP titles.

Andromeda Bookshop Ltd.
Roger G Peyton
United Kingdom
mailorder@andromedabook.co.uk

Bad Moon Books
1854 W. Chateau Ave.
Anaheim, CA 92804
www.badmoonbooks.com

Barry R. Levin Science Fiction &
Fantasy Literature
www.raresf.com

Blood Letting Press and Bookstore
Larry Roberts
www.bloodlettingpress.com

Borderlands Books
866 Valencia St.,
San Francisco CA 94110
888 893-4008
www.borderlands-books.com

Camelot Books and Gifts
6221 Land O' Lakes Boulevard
Land O' Lakes, FL   34639
866-634-9417
www.camelotbook.com

Chris Drumm Books
Cdrummbks@aol.com

Coffee Shop of Horrors
Brice Vorderbrug
www.coffeeshopofhorrors.com
bvorder@aol.com

Cold Tonnage Books - Andy Richards
United Kingdom
andy@coldtonnage.demon.co.uk

Corner Book Store
www.abebooks.com/home/
cornerbookstore

Coven Books - Larry Coven
E-Mail: clovecraft@aol.com

Dark Delicacies
4213 W. Burbank Blvd.,
Burbank, CA 91505
818-556-6660  and  888-darkdel
www.darkdel.com

DreamHaven Books
dreamhvn@visi.com

Necro Publications Bookstore
www.edwardleeonline.com

Other Worlds Bookstore - Paul Dobish
sfbooks@cox.net

Realms of Fantasy Books
ofilip@nstar.net

Shocklines.Com
www.shocklines.com

Mark V. Zeising Bookseller
www.ziesingbooks.com

www.ingramcontent.com/pod-product-compliance
Lightning Source LLC
Chambersburg PA
CBHW020635130626
46552CB00003B/1243